ANDRE GONZALEZ

Replicate

Paul,
Thanks for the
support!

First edition

ISBN: 978-0-9977548-9-6

Cover art by Dane Low
Editing by Teja Watson

This book was professionally typeset on Reedsy.
Find out more at reedsy.com

For Arielle and Felix.
Always see a project through its end, and you just might surprise yourself!

"I've demonstrated there's no difference between me and everyone else! All it takes is one bad day to reduce the sanest man alive to lunacy. That's how far the world is from where I am. Just one bad day."

–The Joker, *Batman: The Killing Joke*

Contents

1

Chapter 1

Jeremy Heston may have avoided jail time, but he was still very much in prison. When he arrived at Rocky Mountain Mental Health Institute on Thanksgiving day, they rushed him into a back room, not much bigger than a closet, and immediately placed him in a straitjacket.

A monstrous black man with biceps as large as Jeremy's torso stood guard while two doctors fastened the straps on the straitjacket and scribbled notes on a clipboard.

"Okay, Mr. Heston, I believe we're ready," said the short doctor in a squeaky voice. The light glared off the bald spot he was trying to hide underneath his thinning comb-over.

Jeremy attempted to move his arms, but the compression of the straitjacket made it impossible. His arms were crossed below his rib cage and would apparently stay there for a while.

"This is more of a precaution," the other doctor said. He was tall and bony, but still had a full head of thick brown hair.

"How long do I need to be in this?" Jeremy asked. After spending the last two years acting insane, he now needed to flip the script and act normal. Aside from meetings with his defense attorney, Linda, he had lacked social interaction over the last two years. Talking to himself grew old, and when the man in the shadows visited him in his jail cell, that's when Jeremy knew it was time to get out.

"Until Dr. Carpenter downgrades your status. It's common procedure for someone in your predicament." The tall doctor explained this, his droopy eyes suggesting he had seen some shit in the loony bin.

My predicament? You mean a mass murderer who walked away from it all as an innocent man. Jeremy fought off a smirk.

"When do I meet Dr. Carpenter?" Jeremy asked.

"She won't be in until Monday. She has a long weekend for the holiday break."

Four days in this shit? Fuck.

"Now, Mr. Heston, if you'll allow us to guide you to your room, we can get you settled in and explain your stay with us. Please follow us."

The short doctor left the room without a word, followed by the tall doctor. The security man, whose name badge read COOPER, placed a surprisingly gentle hand on Jeremy's shoulder and directed him out of the room.

They walked down a long hallway, passing multiple closed doors that Jeremy assumed belonged to other patients. He always imagined a mental hospital as a miserable place: dim lighting, pissed off guards, dirty walls, and shitty food. Prison, basically. He was glad to be proven wrong.

The facility appeared more like an assisted living home: immaculate carpeting, bright lights, nurses and guards with wide smiles. Before they reached the end of the hall, where the doctors called an elevator, Jeremy caught a glimpse of a community room with board games, a TV, and a group of people playing cards around a coffee table. Behind the room was a door that led outside to a small courtyard. It was a cold day, so no one was outdoors, but Jeremy hoped he would get actual time in nature after being cooped up inside for the last two years.

The elevator doors parted as Jeremy and Cooper arrived and they stood together as the doctors stood to the sides facing each other. Jeremy glanced at the neon red number inside as the elevator rose multiple floors. A bell chimed as it flashed a 5 and the doors opened.

Another long hallway greeted them and the doctors immediately started down it. The lights on this floor flickered suspiciously, revealing light, cream-colored walls and a handful of doors spaced apart. They walked to the last door, where the tall doctor jiggled a key in the lock and pushed it open.

Jeremy entered the room and squinted as the brightness blinded him. White padding covered every inch of the room except for the lone window that stood ten feet above a bed pushed in the corner.

Sheets! A comforter and pillow!

He had acclimated to sleeping on a cot, but the thought of a real bed made him feel like a king. A couch awaited on the opposite side of the bed, but that was it.

"Where do I go to the bathroom?" he asked, used to having his toilet within five steps at all times.

"Please have a seat, Jeremy," the short doctor said and gestured to the couch. He held his clipboard and crossed off something with a hard stroke of his pen.

"What are your names?" Jeremy demanded.

"I'm Dr. Mullin," the short doctor said. "And that is Dr. Holtzman. You won't see too much of us, but we may assist Dr. Carpenter at times. She's the head psychiatrist at the hospital and you'll meet with her nearly every day."

Dr. Holtzman cut in, "She's the sole person in charge of making decisions like when you can get out of that jacket."

"Does she decide when I can go home?" Jeremy asked.

The doctors stared at each other with raised eyebrows. "We'll let Dr. Carpenter discuss the discharge process with you," Dr. Holtzman said. "Now, please, let's move on. You may have noticed we came to the fifth floor; this is the top floor of the building. You're in the furthest room from the elevator and stairs. This is because you're a maximum security threat. Should you somehow find a way out of this room, alarms will go off and you will be tranquilized immediately.

"Meals and restroom breaks will be handled by a nurse. We have a team of nurses who will rotate to feed you and help you use the bathroom. Obviously, in a straitjacket you can't do much on your own. Once you're out of the jacket, you'll be feeding yourself and using the restroom in your permanent room on the fourth floor. For now your meals will be at 7 a.m., noon, and 6 p.m. A nurse will check with you every two hours to see if you need to use the restroom. That is how the next four days will go and possibly more, depending on Dr. Carpenter's decision. Questions?"

Jeremy nodded. "What am I supposed to do?"

"Nothing," Dr. Mullin said. For a doctor he sure was a prick.

"This will be hard at first," Dr. Holtzman, the compassionate one, said. "You're confined to this room and your jacket until otherwise instructed. Once you're deemed safe, you'll have more activities you can do."

"Will I get to mingle with others?"

"That's much further down the road, and again at the discretion of Dr. Carpenter."

"Anything else?" Dr. Mullin asked.

"I guess not," Jeremy said. *Guess I'll sit here and stare at the wall for four days. I can't even fondle myself in this damn jacket.*

"Perfect. Lindsay, our head nurse, will be in to introduce herself to you later and let you know a little more on what to expect from the nurses. We'll see you later."

The doctors exited the room with Cooper, who had stood silently by the open door the whole time. The door closed and Jeremy listened as the lock bolted shut, trapping him in the room against his will.

This is prison, he thought. *Only they don't call it that because I have a real bed and padded walls to not injure my crazy self.*

He stood in the middle of the room and stared at the window above him. A glimpse of the gray sky was all he could see. For all he knew, he could be on another planet. He longed for the chance to roam more than a confined space.

Dr. Carpenter seems to be the key to everything.

He noticed a camera in the top corner beside the window.

They're watching me. I'll probably be under constant surveillance my whole time here.

Jeremy had achieved his goal of obtaining the insanity verdict, but felt more of a prisoner than before. For so long, the trial had seemed to be his biggest obstacle, but now he saw that the trial was elementary compared to the challenge of trying to get out of this place.

Chapter 2

Connor Chappell spent his Thanksgiving night on the Internet, researching every bit of information available about Rocky Mountain Mental Health Institute. The news had mentioned that Jeremy Heston had been transported to the mental hospital. He had returned from spending the afternoon with his parents, but no one felt like eating turkey.

Just when they thought they'd be able to move on from the loss of their family's youngest member, Charlie, the brainwashed jury decided to set his killer free. The decision the week prior had reopened the wounds that had never fully healed.

Thanksgiving 2017 was supposed to be spent celebrating Charlie's killer rotting on death row. Instead, the bullshit excuse of mental health let the fucker off the hook.

"I'll make it right, Charlie," Connor said in his empty apartment. He had childhood pictures scattered on his kitchen table, where he sat with an open laptop. His kid brother didn't deserve this, none of the victims did. Charlie had loved his job and often bragged to Connor about how fun it was, sending him selfies taking shots of vodka from his desk. Connor worked in construction, specializing in demolition.

Connor had celebrated his thirty-second birthday in Las Vegas with his brother, only two months before his death in March of 2014. That trip felt like decades ago.

The months following Charlie's murder led to a downward spiral in which Connor consoled himself with alcohol, cocaine, LSD, and anything that didn't require poking himself with a needle.

The thought of having a normal life again vanished when the verdict came back as not guilty. There was too much work to do while that fucker lived a cushy life in the hospital with no regrets. Heavy bags formed under his bloodshot eyes while the drugs took their toll on his once-chiseled body. He managed to keep his job through all the shit. Blowing shit up while strung out on coke was a match made in heaven.

He lit a cigarette as he stared at a picture of him and Charlie from more than twenty years ago. Connor was Batman, Charlie was Robin. The dynamic duo of two blond boys from Littleton, Colorado, stood with their chests puffed out and their twig arms flexed, in the front yard of their childhood home. His parents sold the place after Charlie was killed.

Connor stood from the table and walked to the front door, where he had pinned Jeremy Heston's mugshot. "It's a daily reminder that a piece of shit can ruin everything," he had explained to his parents when they questioned the disturbing picture during a visit. The man in the picture had long, wavy hair splayed out in a mess, wide eyes, and a smirk of evil. He looked every bit as crazy as the liberal doctors said he was, but Connor knew it was all bullshit. Only guilty cowards hid behind an insanity defense.

He blew smoke at the picture. "You're going to pay for what

7

you did." Connor smiled, inhaled more smoke, and blew it back at the picture. "I'm not resting until your body's cold in the ground." He returned to the laptop.

After a week of intensive research, Connor had concluded that getting into the hospital would be nearly impossible. Only close relatives, doctors, and legal representatives were allowed to visit patients, and that was once they were cleared for visitation. Jeremy wouldn't likely receive visitation rights for quite some time. He might, however, receive clearance for outdoor time, and that would be Connor's chance.

The hospital wasn't isolated like a prison. It was a block away from a shopping center, and there were other surrounding buildings on the medical campus. A look at the satellite map of the area showed a few places Connor could perch with a rifle. He'd need to refresh his skills, as it would be a long-distance shot, but he knew he could do it.

The main issue was the distance to Pueblo. It was at least a two hour drive from his home in Denver, and with all the California hipsters moving to town, traffic was always a problem, making the drive closer to two hours on a good day.

Working in construction, he could request work in Pueblo. He could rent a shithole to live in for a couple months until the project completed, and find time to visit the shooting range, to practice his accuracy with his hunting rifle. He would need to scope out the possible spots he could shoot from as well, requiring a clear view to the hospital's courtyard, tucked behind the back of the building.

Whatever it takes, Connor thought as he pulled the map of the hospital back up on his screen, a picture of a young Charlie smiling at him from the table.

3

Chapter 3

The weekend had been even more torturous than Jeremy had feared. The weather cleared up on Friday morning, brightening the room the rest of the weekend. The constant reflection off the white padded walls gave him a headache. Jeremy spent most of his days lying on the couch with his eyes closed.

Mary remained a comforting presence in this version of hell, along with the two other nurses, Molly and Tanya, who tended to him. They lacked Mary's charm, but were helpful and patient, clearly trained under the steady hand of the head nurse.

When Jeremy woke on Monday morning, he had still not grown used to his arms being strapped down. He was impressed by the straitjacket—after four whole days tied in it he still couldn't do more than wiggle his fingers and flex his arms, which were surely losing the bulk he had built up before leaving jail.

Mary returned Monday after having the weekend off, and fed Jeremy a breakfast of eggs, toast, and orange juice. The good food hadn't gotten old and probably never would.

"Today's a big day for you," Mary said after he finished

eating. "Dr. Carpenter will be up here at 10 a.m."

"Anything I should know about her?" Jeremy asked.

"I've worked with more doctors than I can count, and let me tell you, Dr. Carpenter is in the top five. She's fair, kind, and one of the smartest people I've ever met. All doctors are smart, but with her it's different."

"I see." He hoped she wouldn't be intimidating after months of harassment in jail. Dr. Carpenter held the keys to his future, and he needed to impress her.

"I'll let you get back to it," Mary said. "Relax before the doc comes to meet you."

I've had a stressful day hugging myself, I suppose I do need a nap.

Mary gathered the tray with his dirty dishes and exited the room. The sunlight again blinded him, so he lay down on the couch, resting his feet on the arm.

His mind wandered outside the walls that confined him. Why hadn't he heard from his parents? Surely they had to be happy with the verdict and would want to see their son. Maybe they couldn't yet, but why hadn't they visited during his final week in jail after the trial?

He had plenty to ponder, but the rattle of the door interrupted his thoughts. Was it already 10 o'clock?

A pudgy woman walked in, pristine white lab coat draped from her shoulders to her knees.

"Jeremy?" she asked, a smile on her round face as she closed the door and strolled toward Jeremy.

"Dr. Carpenter? Nice to finally meet you," Jeremy said.

"The pleasure is all mine. How has it been since you arrived?" She sat on the bed across from his couch.

"Aside from being tied up, it's been alright. Been getting a lot of headaches from the lighting."

"It's funny how that one little window can illuminate such a big room." Dr. Carpenter spoke with concise enunciation on each word. "Before I go into anything, are there any questions you've been waiting to ask me?"

"Yes. When do I get out of this jacket?"

"Possibly tonight, maybe tomorrow. I'll be doing an analysis today on your current state of mind, but after speaking with the doctors who worked with you during the trial, you should have your high-risk status dropped by midweek at the latest."

"Great. When can I go outside?"

"You won't be allowed outside until you're cleared to mingle with other patients. I'll need to do some tests to determine your ability to socialize and be a productive citizen of the hospital."

"What do you mean by 'productive citizen'?" Jeremy asked.

"Well, Jeremy, every patient in this hospital is, like you, looking for mental healing. One of the biggest steps a patient can take toward being reintroduced to society is to show improved social skills here in the hospital first. Down on the first floor we have events almost every day of the week, all of them put on by the patients."

"Is there anyone else trapped in a padded room?"

"I can't share that information, but I don't expect you to be in here much longer."

"When can I go home?"

Dr. Carpenter paused, looked at the floor, and scratched her head through short, reddish hair.

"I don't know that you'll be going home," she said flatly.

Jeremy's brow furrowed. "Why not?"

"Jeremy, you killed thirteen people and wounded dozens more. While I'm on your side for the road to recovery, I'll be honest...violent offenders like yourself almost never receive clearance to leave." Her tone had softened from authoritative to comforting. "I'd say if it's possible, it would be in fifty years or so, long after I'm gone."

The words hung in the air.

What kind of fucked-up process is that? I was let off fair and square.

"So the not guilty verdict doesn't really mean anything."

"You have to understand that it's as much about your safety as it is others'. If you were let out of here tomorrow, the public would attack you and probably kill you. There were miniature riots after your verdict was announced. People were obviously not happy."

"Sure, but that doesn't seem right. If I can recover, I should be able to get back in the world."

"I agree, but this isn't a simple process. I can guarantee that I will always remain fair. I don't hold your actions against you. I believe in mental disorders causing actions similar to yours, and so did the jury. Believe it or not, I'm on your side. You can set a new precedent. In this era of technology and instant news coverage, you're the first person to receive an insanity verdict after a massacre. It's groundbreaking, and rest assured I'll be handling you with white gloves."

"Are you supposed to be saying this to me?" Jeremy asked.

"Saying what? It's my job to help those with mental disorders. I care deeply for my patients and believe in a strong road to recovery. Do I agree with what you did? Of course not. But I also believe that wasn't the true you. The human mind is more complex than we think and its capabilities are truly infinite. The opportunity to study you is a blessing. We have the rarest of chances to change the future of the mental health field."

"Did you know I was a psychology student before all this?"

"Of course, which only adds an interesting facet to the mix."

"So is there some sort of plan? A schedule?"

"Not so much, but we can get started now. I'll be asking you a series of yes or no questions. That's all you need to respond with."

"Okay."

She pulled a pen out of her pocket and flipped open the file to a sheet with a checklist of questions.

"Do you have any regrets?"

"Yes."

"Do you have any violent urges?"

"No."

"Have you thought about hurting yourself in the last month?"

He thought back to the night in his jail when he wrapped the sheet around his neck and pulled as hard as he could. He had known it wouldn't kill him, but wanted to see, just in case.

"No."

"Have you had any thoughts of harming others in the last month?"

"No."

Jeremy had lost all sense of time since going to jail. A month, a week, even a year all seemed interchangeable at this point in time. He decided to answer the questions based on what he thought a normal person would say.

"Have you had any thoughts about killing yourself?"

"No."

The series of questions continued for the next half hour, all trying to reveal the same thing: was Jeremy any danger to himself or the staff? He assumed this to be the test to decide if he'd get to escape the straitjacket.

"I'm impressed. I don't see that you pose a threat to anyone at this point in time. I do need to consult with the other doctors before we grant any sort of clearance. In the meantime, I'll continue your prescription to treat the bipolar disorder. Did the drugs ever have any negative side effects for you in jail?"

"No." Jeremy loved the high they provided.

"Great, you'll continue on those at a low dosage. I'll have Mary bring that for you with your breakfast each day. Anything else you need from me?"

"No, doctor, thank you." After a couple of years receiving dirty looks, painfully cold or hot showers, and rude treatment from practically every officer, Jeremy felt out of practice in making any sort of request. Over time he'd probably become comfortable with it, but for now he still felt like a prisoner.

Dr. Carpenter wished him a good day and informed him that she would return at the same time the following day for a follow-up assessment.

Jeremy spent the rest of the day pondering; having nothing to do but stare at the wall had that effect. He wondered if something bigger was at play. He didn't expect to be treated poorly in the hospital, but he also didn't expect a royal welcome from everyone.

Dr. Carpenter seemed excited to have him in her hospital. *Too excited,* he thought. He shook off the thoughts and fantasized about the world outside of his new padded-wall prison.

4

Chapter 4

Wednesday morning, Jeremy knew something was off when Mary hadn't come in with breakfast. She had been prompt every day so far. In the few days in his room, he had learned how to read the shadow cast from the window above to tell the time. It wasn't precise, but he knew it was almost eight o'clock when the rattle finally came from the door.

Dr. Carpenter entered the room with Cooper the security guard.

"Great news, Jeremy. You've officially been downgraded as a security threat and will be moving to the fourth floor, and will have your straitjacket removed."

Jeremy perked up from the couch and stood on excited legs. He was grateful to move on to the next phase of his experiment, despite everything in the hospital being out of his control. Problem-solving would be the main focus as he advanced to different "levels" in the hospital. The news this morning provided confirmation that he had achieved the first level, and now he would slowly start to gain trust from others around the building. Mary and Dr. Carpenter already loved him, and he hadn't even had to turn on the charm.

"Am I leaving now?" he asked, trying to hide his urge to scream in joy.

"Yes, Mary is arranging to have your breakfast sent to your new room. Cooper will escort you and remove your jacket once you're there."

"This way, Mr. Heston." Cooper spoke for the first time, in a deep baritone.

Jeremy shuffled his feet toward the large man and was guided by his hand on Jeremy's shoulder, while Dr. Carpenter trailed a couple paces behind. The hallway had a stinging smell of cleaning chemicals likely used to polish the shiny floors. They took the elevator down one floor, where the new hallway looked no different than the fifth floor. Even the lights flickered the same way.

They passed more closed doors. "You're not alone on this floor, just so you know," Dr. Carpenter said. "You'll still be at the end of the hall, though." She wore high heels that clicked and echoed with each step toward the end of the hall. She stepped in front of Jeremy and Cooper when they arrived at the door and pushed it open.

No more padded walls!

Alternate shades of green decorated the walls. Two windows had views to the outside world: one facing the Rocky Mountains, one facing the other buildings on campus. The bed was tucked in the same corner, as was the couch. A table where Jeremy could actually sit and eat a meal stood in the middle of the room, along with a porcelain toilet to the left of the door.

They worked their way to the middle of the room. "Please face me, Mr. Heston," Cooper said.

Jeremy turned and Cooper's massive hands reached out to tug on different belts on the straitjacket. After a few seconds of the guard wrestling with the complex jacket, Jeremy felt the release of tension as his arms fell to his sides. He raised his hands and examined them as if they were a new feature on his body.

"Thank God," he said.

"Anything else from me, Dr. Carpenter?" Cooper asked. She had spread out papers across the table.

"No, sir, thank you for your help," she said with a smile and Cooper left the room. "Now, Jeremy, this is a big step. I hope you understand, you're not in the clear yet. Any misstep and you'll be back on the fifth floor. Understood?"

Jeremy nodded. "So what happens now?"

"You may be in this room for a while. The next month will consist of heavy testing, mostly by me, but there will be some other doctors stopping in from time to time as well. As far as how you can progress, it will be in steps. As you see, you now have a full room. In time, we'll grant you things like books and puzzles to help get your mind back on track. Your brain has probably softened the last two years in jail, but we can recover its acuity. Eventually, you'll be granted permission to spend supervised time outside. Once you receive clearance to mingle with other patients, it will be on a limited basis, one hour per week, and will gradually increase as you improve. At some point you'll be a full participant with all community activities in the hospital."

"How long does this all take?"

"Depends on how your tests go. Could be months or years. It's a process that takes into account many opinions before final decisions are made."

"And this can all lead to one day going home?"

"Jeremy, you need to let that thought go. At one point you'll

17

be granted visitation rights and we can see about getting your parents to come see you. Bringing home to you. You won't be leaving."

Jeremy sunk in his chair. Why was the doctor so nice and genuine, but adamant on him never leaving? Wasn't the point of the mental institute to rehabilitate the mind so one could re-enter society? It was starting to seem like a big lie.

Remember this stuff for the book.

"You're going to enjoy your time here, I promise. There are great doctors and patients. This is your new home, soon you'll start seeing that."

"I'm gonna die here, aren't I?" Jeremy asked bluntly.

"You'll die in this room if you don't get your mind off the distant future and focus on the present. You need to take this one day at a time. Soon enough, life will feel normal again."

Jeremy shriveled within himself, silent as he had always been when faced with the cold hard truth.

"Okay," he said finally. "Let's get started."

So they began. Dr. Carpenter drilled Jeremy with chronological questions, starting in his childhood. She referred to this as the foundation of all the research. Knowing his past could only help explain his recent and future actions. The questioning took him mentally back to jail, when he had answered the same questions two different times with the psychologists that visited him. If fifty hours of interviewing seemed bad, then a lifetime of questioning would be hell.

But Dr. Carpenter wasn't as bad as the court-appointed shrinks. She had a way of lulling him into a trance. He found he wanted to answer more questions, feeling a passion to discuss his life. Mary silently interrupted and served him breakfast, and the questioning continued while he ate.

By the time they finished for the day, Jeremy was still in the fourth grade on his mental timeline. He would try to jump ahead years, feeling elementary school was irrelevant, but Dr. Carpenter kept the questioning focused on moving slowly and steadily through the chronology. There were no deadlines to meet, no court hearings that required certain tasks to be achieved. The only goal was to get Jeremy back to normal, and that required hearing the small details of his childhood.

"I want to thank you for today, Jeremy," the doctor said as she gathered her papers and organized them in a folder. "I've rarely had patients open up about so much on their first full day of interviewing. It's usually like pulling teeth to get people to talk about their past. You're being cooperative and that will certainly be noted in your file."

"Glad I can help," Jeremy said, smirking. "Please believe me when I tell you I intend to get out of here one day, and preferably before I need to wear a diaper to bed. Just saying."

Dr. Carpenter giggled at this, caught off guard by the quick flash of humor from her new patient.

"If you say so, Jeremy. Have a good rest of the day, and I'll see you in the morning."

5

Chapter 5

From an early age, Harriet Carpenter decided to dedicate her life to mental health. Growing up with an alcoholic father and a depressed younger sister, she decided in high school to pursue a profession studying the human mind. Nights hiding under her bed to avoid a flying backhand when Dad came stumbling home made her vow to find a way to combat mental illness.

Her dad's alcoholism grew worse when she went to college. She believed he did it in spite of her, having no pride in his daughter's educational endeavors. She cut ties with him after graduation, when he didn't show up to the ceremony. Harriet's mom and sister attended and gave a typical cover-up excuse for her dad. To this day she didn't understand the constant enabling and lying they did for the man who treated them like shit.

After graduation, she left her hometown for the first time in her life to take a residency at a psychiatry practice in Portland, Oregon. What she learned under Dr. Reynolds helped her grow into who she was today: fair, detailed, and more knowledgeable than those around her.

Once her residency was complete, she opened her own

private practice; that lasted only four years as she encountered the grueling burden of dealing with incompetent staff, payroll, and scheduling. The clerical work took the joy out of the job. She had developed strong rapport with her patients, but when the offer came to work at the Rocky Mountain Mental Health Institute, she jumped at the opportunity.

At the institute, she could practice on the most severe of cases, have a team of nurses, and be part of important decisions, all without the ugliness of running her own business. It took her only one day on the job to know it was her destiny. She belonged there and needed the hospital as much as it needed her.

The months turned into years, and before she knew it she was the head psychiatrist at the hospital, responsible for signing off on all patients and making the final decision on their status. Many of the doctors who worked for her sought employment elsewhere—not out of spite, but because they knew she was a fixture at the institute. None of them would be getting the opportunity to take her spot.

As painful as the good-byes were, Dr. Carpenter enjoyed hiring her own staff of doctors. She called many friends from college who were still practicing. None had any interest in moving to Pueblo, Colorado, but many did have hungry interns and resident students they vouched for. Harriet found most of them to be very qualified, perfect for what she was looking for. After two months of interviews, she had her hand-picked team to lead the way into the future for the institute.

"The future is today," she had told them on their first day of orientation. She'd always had a drive to make things better, and her running of the hospital proved no different. With a new staff, Dr. Carpenter asked the state for funds to renovate the building, which they surprisingly approved. Perhaps they also recognized it as the next era of mental health care in Colorado.

Her system took a couple years to fully implement, but once it was the hospital became one of the most respected in the region. High-profile defendants started to receive their sentencing to the hospital, many from out of state, and Dr. Carpenter welcomed them with open arms.

When the news broke of Jeremy Heston and his mass slaughtering of innocent lives, even she had dismissed the possibility of him one day being admitted under her care. Juries never let off a mass murderer, and his case would be no different.

That all changed when she received a phone call the evening before the trial's closing arguments. An old friend from college, Adrian, had called her to discuss an important matter.

"I can get you Jeremy Heston," her friend said in a hushed voice.

"What do you mean?" she asked. Her internal sensors were going off. Something wasn't right about the call.

"I know you want to study that beautiful mind of his. So do I. We'll never be able to do that if he's in jail."

We? Was Adrian inviting himself to come work with her as a volunteer? There were no job openings.

"Are you on the jury? How can you be so sure?"

"I'm not on the jury, but I've been to every day of the trial. I've studied the jury. Some of them are actually leaning toward an acquittal. I don't know much about law, but I know how to read people. Trust me."

Her interest was piqued at the possibility. "Okay, but you sound confident you can get Heston to me. How?"

"The less you know the better, but I can get him for you."

"And what's in it for you?"

"All I want is the opportunity to study him with you. I have a private practice. I'll never get an opportunity like this. Twenty-four hour access to the most intriguing patient in the history of psychology. I want in."

Most intriguing? That's a stretch, she thought. But Adrian wasn't wrong. Heston was the yeti of psychology. If these mass murderers didn't take their own lives after their attacks, they always ended up in prison for life. Mass shooters never had the chance to be studied, but here was opportunity knocking on history's door.

Worst-case scenario, she'd have a new patient who would spend his life in her care. The best case was unlimited, with possible legislation changes in mental health at the forefront of her mind. She could write books about studying the mind of the most notorious criminal in recent times.

"Okay. I'm interested," she told her friend. "You can guarantee this?" She remained skeptical, but couldn't ignore the confidence in his voice.

"Absolutely. I'm not going to share the details, but I can make it happen—just wanted to make sure you'll let me in on all the fun."

"I can hire you on as a temp tomorrow, get it on the books. I don't need anything looking suspicious on my end."

"Whatever you need to do, Dr. Carpenter." She could hear the smile on his face through the phone. "I'll see you soon."

The phone clicked and he was gone without a good-bye. Dr. Carpenter had taken the call in her office. She swiveled around in her chair to look outside the window overlooking the mountains.

Is this wrong? I'm not even doing anything, technically. I'm not paying him, not bribing him, I didn't even ask him. He asked me.

Even though she hadn't done anything, she still felt slimy. She wanted to study Heston; it would be an opportunity she couldn't deny. But if she watched the verdict come back as not guilty by reason of insanity, she would know it was somehow rigged.

Having never been a cheater, she experienced a new kind of guilt for the first time in her life. Despite it, though, something big was coming her way, and she had to be ready for the pressure and media attention that would surely follow.

"I can handle it," she assured herself.

6

Chapter 6

Robert and Arlene Heston sat on their backyard patio listening to oldies on the radio and sipping lemonade. A sense of reality had yet to return for them, but their move to Flagstaff, Arizona, had helped get them back on track. They had always saved aggressively for retirement and now had more than enough to call it quits.

"We have to go back. He's our son," Arlene said.

Robert stared at his lemonade, poured a splash of vodka in it, and sipped it without acknowledging his wife. She had nagged him all week about a return visit to Colorado.

"Dr. Carpenter said it could be beneficial to his recovery to see us, even just once," Arlene continued. The last two years had brought whiteness and wrinkles to her hair and body; Robert hadn't fared much better.

"I can't do it." Robert's voice cracked. "I can't look him in the eye, just like he couldn't look us in the eye all those days in court. That's not our son anymore."

Robert had reached a point where all he wanted to do was drink and smoke cigars until he died. His son's shooting rampage had sucked the life out of him.

"We have to," Arlene said. Robert had heard those three words at least fifty times over the last two days, since Dr. Carpenter called to inform them that Jeremy had been cleared for immediate-family visitation rights.

"You can go by yourself if you must," Robert said nonchalantly.

"Rob, he's *our* son. Our only son. We have to both be there for him."

"Be there? We've always been there for him, and he still goes and kills his entire office. We don't owe him shit!"

Arlene's eyes welled with tears. "I hate him, too, you know. I'll never forgive him. I still remember the night before, when he came over for dinner. Why couldn't he have just told us what was wrong? None of this would've happened."

"Let it go."

"No. That was the last time everything was normal. I'm not saying we need to visit him every month. I just want to go one time, to get closure. I'm not going to leave this life without saying good-bye to my only son. You shouldn't either."

"My son is as good as dead to me."

"Rob, he's sick."

"Bull-fucking-shit! Don't tell me you buy into this mentally insane shit. You know our son has never been mentally ill. It's all bullshit from this new generation. They are literally coddling a mass murderer by calling him sick."

"Did you want him to die, Rob?"

"At this point, I don't care anymore. At the time, no, I didn't want him to die. But every day that goes by and I think back on it, I care less. He killed all those people for no reason."

Arlene bolted back in her lounge chair. Robert poured more vodka into his cup. This same argument had become a daily occurrence as they settled in to their new home in Flagstaff.

"I'm not stopping you from going and getting your closure. I don't need closure. Jeremy might as well be dead, because I'm not going to see him again."

Arlene shook her head. "Fine. Then I'll go by myself to see our *only* child. Hope you don't get too drunk and crack your head on your goddamn hot tub." She jumped from her chair and stomped her way inside, slamming the door with authority.

Robert stared into the sky as if nothing had happened. The fights had been constant since the shooting, after a couple months of mourning and accepting what their son had done. Leaving Colorado became a necessity, as they both no longer felt welcome. Lifelong neighbors stopped talking to them, and they received dirty looks around town.

Jeremy had also ended their lives as they knew them.

Robert spent a week cooped up in his office, running numbers from their savings account to see what their options were. They had never planned to leave Colorado for a warm location like most retirees, but now they had no option. Arizona was close enough to Denver, should they ever need to visit other family, but also far enough away that they could start a new life. The cost of living was also significantly cheaper, and Robert had no issues with not having to work another day in his now-miserable life.

Vodka lemonades had become his breakfast and lunch, while a six pack of beer washed it all down for dinner. When he was sober all he could think about was sitting in court, visiting Jeremy, and picturing the massacre left behind by the hands of his son. He had seen all the crime scene photos and wouldn't ever be able to erase them from his memory. Instead, the constant alcohol kept his mind in a numbed state, where he could feel relaxed and enjoy the scorching hot nature around him; 110-degree afternoons weren't so bad when you couldn't feel anything but the booze swirling in your stomach.

Arlene could go by herself. He understood her angle, but he'd be damned if he'd look at his son again. Seeing him would only remind him of all the shit that had spiraled out of control since the shooting. Numbness in Arizona was all he could handle, and he intended to keep it that way.

* * *

Back in Denver, Connor Chappell stood in the office of his project director, Pete Sandoval. Pete was known as a no-nonsense man who wore the same rotation of flannel shirts every week, and kept his hard hat on at all times as if it held his head together.

"You want to take an extended job in Pueblo?" he asked Connor, brushing bread crumbs from his thick black mustache. "Why?"

They had developed a good working relationship over the years. Connor was his main go-to whenever a new project needed a supervisor to get the ball rolling.

"I'm just becoming fed up with the city. I need to get away."

"Is this about the promotion?" Pete asked.

Connor had been passed up on a promotion the week prior for a move into a project management role. He would have received a $20,000 increase in salary, along with a whole new level of responsibility. He had wanted the job, interviewed for it, and been turned down in favor of someone who had only been on the job for a year. Connor held no hard feelings, though, as his mind was dedicated to avenging his brother's death.

"Not at all."

"Is this about your brother?" Pete sipped a coffee mug that read THE ROAD TO SUCCESS IS ALWAYS UNDER CONSTRUCTION.

"Kinda. March will be the two-year anniversary and I'd rather not be here. My family's miserable to be around, and if I can just be away, I can clear my head and refocus on my career."

"You have been slacking, I've noticed. Fortunately, your version of half-ass work is still better than most people's best. But I know what you're capable of."

Connor said nothing and held eye contact with Pete.

"Okay. I'll take you on. Perhaps a change of scenery will get you back where I know you can be. Rumor is there will be another PM position next summer. If you can get back to your normal self, I don't see any reason for you to be passed over again."

Pete turned in his chair to face his computer monitor and started clicking. "We have a job in Pueblo starting the first week of January. Would run six months and wrap up in June. Is that about what you're looking for?"

"That would be perfect." Connor grinned and felt a fluttering in his stomach.

"Alright, it's yours. I'll mark you as the lead supervisor for the project. It's an extension of the main shopping mall. Mostly adding more parking spots, but there'll be some work needed on the building itself."

"I don't mind that one bit. Who doesn't love the mall?"

The fluttering turned into a tingling sensation. Connor knew the area well. The mall was two blocks away from the Rocky Mountain Mental Health Institute.

7

Chapter 7

"Christmas is next week, and every year we have a big celebration on Christmas Eve, where all the patients and nurses come together for a party put on by the patients." Dr. Carpenter sat across from Jeremy at his table, a grin on her face.

The last three weeks of interviewing had gone well. They had covered his chronological timeline in the first week and then had started to dive deeper into specific issues. The doctor seemed to enjoy grilling him on matters regarding his past employment. Maybe she thought she could find something that tied all of this together. He had talked more about the Denver Bears than he would have thought possible.

"Very cool, is that something I'll get to go to?" Jeremy asked, trying to tamper the excitement creeping up to his throat.

"I haven't decided yet. We're typically more lax than normal about granting permission for the holiday party, but you're definitely infamous around the hospital. The other patients know who you are. I'm not sure if that's good or bad, but it may be distracting to have your first public appearance be the party."

"Then let me meet some of the other patients," Jeremy

pleaded. His only relationships in the last two years had been with his attorney and psychologists. The loneliness made him wonder if he would even be able to carry on a conversation with someone not obsessed with his past.

"I'm not ready to give you that kind of clearance. Should I grant you permission to attend the party, it would be with a nurse by your side the entire time, possibly a security guard as well."

"I thought I wasn't a threat anymore."

"You're not classified as a threat, but there have been drastic reactions in the past at the reintroduction to social life. I've told you I'll always be up front with you, though, and this is what I'm thinking at the moment. I'll be considering it over the next week, but may not make a final decision until Christmas Eve morning."

"Okay. If it counts for anything, I'd really like the chance, even if it's just for a limited time."

One thing had become apparent as he started to mentally prepare for an escape plan: he needed a confidant in the hospital, preferably one who had been there a long time. Not a nurse, not a doctor, not a guard. None of them would ever stoop to his level. He needed a fellow patient, someone who knew the ins and outs of the hospital, someone whose trust he could gain, who would have no issue helping him devise a plan. That would never happen if he couldn't meet the other patients.

"It doesn't count for anything, but thanks for trying. I did want to let you know that there will be a new doctor coming to see you in January. He's an old friend of mine and was looking for some temporary work."

"Lovely," Jeremy said sarcastically. The rotation of doctors had worn him out. Every week a new hotshot doctor strolled in thinking they could crack the case of Jeremy Heston's mind, and every week they left with their tails tucked between their legs in a figurative failure. None of them had tried to connect with Jeremy like Dr. Carpenter did. She could ask him anything and he obliged with a straight response. The other doctors made him feel defensive, so he tended to give vague answers. Dr. Carpenter knew this, but didn't care to call him out on it.

"You're progressing. I have no issue with you getting books at this time. Is there anything in particular you'd like to read?"

"I'd rather write. Can I get some sort of journal?"

Dr. Carpenter hesitated before answering. "Not yet. Writing works a much different part of the brain that we haven't quite covered. I'll make note that you have interest, though. What would you write about?"

"Either a diary or short stories. Never had the stamina to write books. Just stuff I can crank out in an hour or two."

"I see." She scribbled a note.

"On second thought, I'll take a copy of *The Shawshank Redemption*, so I can find out how to chisel my way out of here." He intended for it to sound sarcastic and it must have worked, based on the grin that took over the doctor's face.

"Very funny," she said. "I'll see that we get you a copy. One of my favorites."

"Thank you. I was also wondering why I haven't had any visitors yet."

The doctor clicked her pen before dropping it on top of his file. "I couldn't tell you."

"Where are my parents? I have a hard time believing they wouldn't come see me."

"Did they ever visit you in jail?"

"A couple times, yes."

"Last I heard, they were in Arizona. Had they mentioned that to you?"

"No. They hardly talked to me when they came to visit in jail. My dad couldn't even look at me."

"I think we should call it a day," she said, standing as she collected the folder.

"Your call, Dr. Carpenter. I'm here all day if you need me."

She left, white lab coat swaying behind her, without saying another word.

Did I get to her? Jeremy wondered. He'd thought it impossible to affect the head doctor in any way, but she had just left him without speaking, something she had never done.

Jeremy had not been taking his pills; a week prior he had started dissolving the pills in his mouth and spitting out the mush once the nurse left. It didn't take long before he felt less fatigued and able to have deeper thoughts. He had enjoyed his clear mind, feeling it return to the sharpness it had once had. He thought back to his notebook, now sitting in a landfill in the middle of nowhere. It would be the perfect book to write an escape plan in, like reuniting with an old friend.

Instead, his mental checklist would have to suffice. With his wits returning and the resurrection of his workout plan (which now no longer needed to be done in the middle of night), he knew it would just be a matter of timing and learning the facility before something concrete could be put in place and executed.

"You will get out of here," he whispered to himself. "Just stay ready."

8

Chapter 8

Christmas passed without Jeremy being granted permission to attend the party. He remained isolated in his room while the rest of the building attended the party on Christmas Eve. He wondered if it was a test by Dr. Carpenter, to see how he would react to the rejection. Rejection was, after all, what led him down the path to the loony bin.

She explained that while she believed he would be fine attending the party, it wasn't the right time, and he would be granted permission to mingle with other patients soon. Perhaps it was all part of her plan. If it was, good for her for staying many steps ahead. Even though his mind felt almost back to full strength, his knowledge of psychology remained too rusty to join the chess match against Dr. Carpenter.

"This is bullshit," he said calmly to himself the night of the party. He could see glowing lights splayed across the dark campus. *Do they have a disco ball?* he wondered, feeling anger creep in. He hadn't felt a deep sense of rage since the fateful day in 2016, and he didn't intend to let it get a hold of him again. Maybe he would take his next pill, rather than just pretending to, to take the edge off; they always relaxed him.

Jeremy stood at his window, watching the flashing lights brighten the ground four stories below him. A few lights glowed across the blacked-out horizon of Pueblo. When he looked up, he saw a familiar face in the reflection of the window and felt his blood instantly freeze.

The black-haired man stood stiffly in his usual black suit, hands crossed in front of his crotch.

"Hi, Jeremy. Looks like you're doing well," he said in a cold voice.

Jeremy turned sharply, hoping his mind was playing tricks with the reflection, but the man stood there unfazed. He picked up and examined the copy of *Rita Hayworth and Shawshank Redemption* that rested on the table.

"What do you plan on doing when you escape from here?" the man asked nonchalantly.

"I can't escape from here," Jeremy snapped. He was sick of this man showing up and never explaining himself.

"I'm sure it'll happen."

"Tell me who you are. You're obviously not real. No one could have gotten in here so easily."

"On the contrary." The man grinned, revealing yellowed teeth, and pulled out a set of janitor keys from his suit pocket, dangling from his long, bony fingers. "I'm very persuasive and can usually find my way into any place."

"What do you want?" Jeremy felt his heart rate increasing and wondered if the man could sense his panic.

"You keep asking, and I'll never tell. You'll know one day who I am, but until then it doesn't really matter. What I can tell you is that you have big things ahead. Remember the last time we spoke?"

"Yes, you told me I'd kill again. Hate to break it to you, but that's not the point of all this. I did this to expose this country's issues with mental health."

"How can you expose anything when you're crazy? Who would take you serious?"

"I'm not crazy."

"You're no different than the homeless guys downtown, talking to the walls. You've got a few screws loose, my friend." The man twirled a finger beside his head while he smirked. "They diagnosed you as bipolar, did you forget that?"

"Nope. When I get out of here, I'm gonna write a book."

"A book?" the man gasped. "A book about what?"

"About mental health and why it needs to be taken seriously."

The man grabbed his flat stomach and cackled, throwing his head back in a violent motion.

"I never knew you could be so funny," he said. "Your grand plan was to murder your coworkers, go to court, pray by some miracle to get sentenced to a mental hospital so that you could one day escape to write a book about it? So that the rest of the world could hear how mental health is a real issue?"

It sounded silly hearing it put that way, but Jeremy wasn't going to let this monster put a damper on his plans.

"Yes, that's exactly it."

The guy in the suit laughed again, this time with more control.

"You've got ambition, Jeremy, I've never doubted that. But this plan is ludicrous. Who's gonna publish or buy a book from you? You're a monster, remember?"

"I don't need your approval. You won't even tell me who or what you are!"

"Remember who you are, Jeremy. You've already shown the

world your true colors. Don't try to lie to yourself. Till next time, my friend."

The man turned and strolled calmly to the door, opened it, closed it, and vanished. Jeremy didn't hear the usual racket of the door being locked and ran to it, pulling desperately.

It didn't budge. It was somehow locked without the man locking it. Tears started to run down Jeremy's cheeks for the first time since his early days in jail.

"The next time I see him, I'm killing him," he said to himself as he wiped the moisture off his face. "He's as good as dead."

That's what he wants you do, Jeremy thought. *He's trying to bait you into killing again, can't you see that?*

He wanted to ask the doctors to look at the camera footage and confirm that a man was in his room. If they confirmed it, then perhaps the man was real after all; maybe he planned on helping him escape at some point. If they checked the tapes and saw no man, then Jeremy would appear insane and who knows what decision would be made about him.

He'd have to wait and see. Hopefully someone was watching and would address the situation without Jeremy needing to ask.

* * *

Jeremy didn't have to wait long to find out. He was left alone on Christmas day, with the exception of the nurse visits. But the day after Christmas saw the return of Dr. Carpenter.

She plopped down in the chair and didn't wait for Jeremy to join her at the table before she started speaking.

"Have a good time on Christmas Eve?"

"Yes. Did you?" he responded resentfully.

"The party was good, yes. What were you doing up here?"

"The usual: sitting, reading, thinking about life as a normal man in this big lonely world."

"Cut the act, Jeremy. One of the guards saw you on the security camera. He said it looked like you were talking to yourself, then you charged at the door like a sprinter."

"I was doing my exercise." Jeremy forced confidence into his voice and hoped she bought it. "I do it every day, do you not see that on the camera?"

"Yes, we've seen it. This was one random sprint, after talking to the wall. You can tell me if something's wrong."

So they are watching me every day. They also think I've lost my mind. Must have been a hallucination.

"Dr. Carpenter, is it possible to have hallucinations from being trapped in the same place all day? What's that called again?" He spoke in his professional voice, the one not used since March of 2016, when he was miserable and on the phones all day. The one he used when he had to take shit from Shelly and pretend everything was okay.

"Cabin fever. And yes, it is possible. Have you been having hallucinations?"

"I think so. It happened to me in jail once, and I think it's what happened the other night. Could it be a possible side effect from my medication?" Jeremy was in his professional mode; he felt like a psychologist himself.

"Hallucinations are not a known side effect for this drug. Jeremy, are you sure you're feeling okay? You seem a little off."

"Yes, I promise I'm fine. I think my workout routine is

39

helping me sleep better. I'm feeling more alert since I've started working out again."

"I see." The doctor scribbled on a notepad. "Tell me about the hallucinations."

Jeremy stayed silent for a moment. He could tell the truth, and likely suffer a setback from all the progress he'd made so far. Or he could lie—but lies only led to more lies. It had been a while since he'd needed to break out the old poker skills for bluffing, but what better time than the present?

"Both times I've seen the same thing," he started, focusing on keeping his heart rate down and his stare into the doctor's eyes confident. "An escape. In jail I saw the cell door open. No one was around. It was just me in the middle of the night. I woke up and saw the door open. When I walked up to it and reached out, it was closed again. That was the first time I thought I might actually have some sort of mental problem, but I remembered a lesson on hallucinations in the middle of the night. They can happen right when the brain switches from its sleeping state to awake."

"Two nights ago you weren't asleep."

"Correct, but I saw the same thing. I swore I saw that door swing open, that's why I made a run for it."

"What do you make of that?"

Jeremy paused, not sure of the doctor's angle. Was she actually taking him serious and wanting his opinion? Doubtful. Perhaps she was pulling him along to help get his mind back to normal.

"I think it's been more of a mirage than anything. Like people stranded in the desert seeing water that's not really there."

Dr. Carpenter nodded on her balled-up fist supporting her chin. "That's very interesting."

"Any idea what it means?" Jeremy asked.

"For starters, you have an obvious desire to be back in the real world. You've been asking about your release since you arrived. I'm not surprised your subconscious is tricking you into seeing it as real."

"I intend to be released one day. I know my mind is okay. Things spiraled out of control, you have to believe me."

"I'm not here to argue with you. I'm here to make sure you recover. How many times have we discussed this?"

Jeremy nodded. He'd thought he might have gained an edge over the doctor, but she turned cold toward him whenever he raised the possibility of leaving. She really did intend to keep him locked up in the hospital as long as she was in charge.

This is no different than the corporate world—I can do everything right, but without someone up above having interest in helping me advance, I'm fucked.

"I don't wanna talk any more today. Can we please take a break?" he asked Dr. Carpenter.

"That's fine." She gathered her papers. "Try to get some rest today. We can try again tomorrow."

Jeremy knew how to read people, always had, and it was obvious that the doctor was frustrated, but she did a solid job in hiding it. Her outward patience suggested that this was a common occurrence that she had learned to handle after many years of practice.

She left the room and wished Jeremy a good afternoon.

9

Chapter 9

Connor stood in the lobby of the Langoni Apartment Complex in Pueblo, the closest apartments to the mental institute. The complex was at the edge of the main neighborhood, directly next to the local news station. Roughly 3,000 feet of a dirt field separated the apartment he wanted from the first building on the institute's campus.

The landlord sat behind his cluttered desk and read over Connor's application.

"Yer background good?" The scrawny man was dressed in tight jeans, cowboy boots, and a red flannel shirt. He spoke with a slight twang.

"Yes, sir," Connor said. He had sobered up to meet with the landlord and now felt that may have been the wrong decision. He felt nauseous and had the chills. "I still have my apartment in Denver, just needing a place for the next six months while I'm out here on a job. Rather not drive two hours each way to get to work."

"Indeed, 'specially this time of year," the landlord said, brushing his thick mustache with a chapped finger. "Okay, you can have a room. Studio good?"

"Yes, sir. Do you have anything west-facing? I've got some sleep issues and any extra minutes I can catch on the weekend would do me well."

The landlord clicked around on his computer. "Sure do. Corner unit, a little more spacious, cost an extra twenty per month."

"I'll take it. Thank you, sir."

"I'll put you down. Do you have first and last month's rent available?"

"Yes, let me write you a check." At $500 per month, rent was a third of the cost compared to Denver. Connor could have covered all six months' rent if the cowboy had asked for it.

"Here's your key, don't lose it." The landlord handed it over, and Connor grabbed it with a grin. "All of our studios are on the top floor, take the elevator up to four and you'll be to the right at the end of the hall. Number 420."

"Thank you, sir. I look forward to staying here." *More than you know.*

"Pleasure's all mine, young man. You let me know if you need anything, okay?"

"Will do." They shook hands and Connor left the office toward the elevator.

From outside, the complex appeared rundown, but the inside had clearly undergone a recent remodel, with fresh paint, carpet, and piercing bright lights in the hallways.

When he arrived at his room, he pushed open the door to find new tile in the kitchen, granite counter tops, and more of the brand-new carpet that still housed the fresh odor in its fibers. His living room—which also served as his bedroom—connected with the kitchen and overlooked the news station next door. Across the field he saw the mental institute, and the thought of living so close to Jeremy Heston made every hair on his body stiffen.

"Hello, neighbor," he said menacingly as he crossed the room to look out the window. Cars were parked four levels below, for both the apartments and the news station. The massive satellites pointing to the sky weren't the most attractive of views, but it could have been worse.

The apartment would work just fine. His job started in two weeks, so he'd have to make a trip back to Denver to gather a sleeping bag, clothes, and his rifle.

For today, though, it was already 5 o'clock and a drive to Denver would be too exhausting. His laptop was in the car, along with a couple of blankets. He wanted to start planning right away, and what better way than with a working view of his main target's location.

He retrieved his laptop and lay on the new carpet to begin his work. Furniture wouldn't be completely necessary, but at least a chair would be needed for his future days in the studio. He pulled up the map of his current location and started highlighting possible areas to scout. There had to be a window that would let him see inside the facility. How close could he get before having to cross paths with security?

He had driven by on the main road and didn't see any sort of armed gate to enter the campus. He should be able to get fairly close if needed, at least for his research—though toting a gun on government property would be a sure way to end up inside the building himself.

Connor took a screen shot of the two-block radius surrounding the institute, his apartment on the outer edge. He highlighted the building and marked special areas of interest. It appeared to have an outdoor courtyard, but it was surrounded by the building in a U-shape. There was also a soccer field on the outskirts of the campus. He looked out the window as the sun started to set and could see the field in plain sight.

"I can shoot him from my window if he's ever on that field."

The thought excited him, but he knew better than to get ahead of himself. Was the field even for patients to use? He would have to watch the campus and take note of any outdoor activity. It being winter, they might not have any major outdoor events until the springtime.

Each floor of the hospital had windows that surely belonged to the patients' rooms. Would binoculars suffice, to find which room Heston was staying in? It would be worth a shot.

10

Chapter 10

The calendar flipped to 2018 for Jeremy's sixth week in the mental institute. Monday, January 8 was a day he'd remember as the critical turning point in his life. He had requested (and was granted) a calendar for the upcoming year. Regaining his sense of time seemed minor, but was critical to a complete recovery; he had gone too long without knowing what day it was. A calendar would also help him make a mental escape plan.

He closed his eyes and remembered plotting the shooting, circling March 11 as the day of destiny. Could he plan to escape from the loony bin on March 11, 2018, two years exactly from the time he left thirteen dead, twenty-two injured, and thousands of lives changed?

How romantic that would be. The city would be in a frenzy once the news broke that I escaped.

He had to brush these thoughts aside, but committed to an aggressive target date of March 11 for an escape.

The door rattled open and Dr. Carpenter entered in her usual perky way. She grew irritable as the week progressed, and Jeremy figured he'd be able to use that to his advantage at some point.

Gotta pick up on the little things.

"Jeremy, good morning. How are you?" she asked as she sat at his table.

"Doing good, and yourself, doctor?" he responded cheerily. One thing Jeremy had learned was that the doctor loved having her ego stroked. *Funny how people in positions of power could be won over so easily by simple and constant praise.* Dr. Carpenter had a lot of similarities to Shelly, with the exception of being a cunt, a trait that led to his former director's eventual death.

"I'm great, and I have great news for you today. We're not going to do any more interviews, at least not to the extent you're used to."

"Oh? Why is that?"

"I've upgraded your current status. How do you feel about meeting some other patients in the hospital today?"

Jeremy nodded with a wide grin after realizing what she had said. "That's all I want. People to talk to besides doctors and nurses. No offense."

"None taken. There's free time in the commons area every day from 10-12. It's already 10:30, so we can arrange to have you downstairs by eleven if that works for you."

"Let me check my schedule." Jeremy glanced mockingly at the calendar on his wall. "Looks like I'm all clear for today."

"Very funny. I want you to know, this will be a process. You'll start with an hour today in the commons, and probably for the remainder of the week. Depending how things go, we may increase that time, as well as expand it to other activities. Any questions?"

"Yes. When you say 'how things go,' what do you mean?" Jeremy was no longer afraid to question her decisions.

"Bipolar disorder has many symptoms, one of the main ones being difficulty with social interaction. Because of that, we want to ease you into it. If you show you can handle an hour a day, then we'll consider giving you more opportunities."

Jeremy hated hearing the word *bipolar*. Every time someone called him that, it felt like a nasty slime dripping into his ears.

"So you're gonna be watching me during this hour."

"Very closely. But don't mind me or the other doctors and nurses. Be yourself with the other patients. Get to know them. They are always welcoming and excited to meet new people, and you'll be no different."

"Do any of them know what I did?"

"Unfortunately, yes. Like anywhere, word spreads like wildfire here. Remember, there was a time where your name and face were all over the news outlets and in the papers. We don't sensor information from our patients. We let them watch the news. Word got out that you were coming here. But I don't believe anyone will hold this against you. All the patients are in here for a reason, yours just received publicity."

"Great. I just want to make some friends."

"That's great! Please do. Friendship is a fantastic thing to develop during your time here. I should get going, though, I need to drop off the official paperwork to grant you access. A nurse will be up to escort you down later. We'll talk about your experience later this afternoon."

"Thanks, Dr. Carpenter. I really do appreciate this chance."

"You've earned it. Just keep up the progress."

She stood and left. For the first time in two years Jeremy felt things coming together, and that sense of fate returned.

Time for the next phase of the plan.

* * *

The nurse led Jeremy down to the main lobby. Jeremy hadn't seen it since his first day, when he was hurried through his processing upon arrival. The doors to the front were unguarded and the sight of that freedom made him drool. The lobby had a reception desk, where a young woman sat, lost in her own world. Next to the desk stood a coffee table, surrounded by two sofas. A fireplace crackled and popped in the background, providing Jeremy that taste of the holidays he had missed.

The nurse led Jeremy down a short hallway and hooked a right to the commons room.

At least thirty patients were scattered across the room. Some played card games, others huddled around the TV, and a small group worked intently on a jigsaw puzzle. Nurses and security guards stood around the perimeter and watched over all the activities.

Jeremy had never been one to walk up to a group of people and insert himself, but he had no choice now. No one looked his way, and he couldn't just stand in the background awkwardly.

Here I am, worried about the loonies liking me.

He believed that being the only sane person in a room full of insane people was a clear advantage, like being two steps ahead of everyone else.

Remember to stick to the plan. You need smart friends. Crazy doesn't mean dumb.

He crossed the commons to the back corner, where three companions rested their hands on the table as they scavenged for the correct pieces for their jigsaw puzzle.

"Hey, guys," Jeremy greeted.

49

Two of the men remained focused on the puzzle, while the other looked up at Jeremy with a look of confusion. "Hi, Jeremy," he said as if he'd known him for years. His blond hair was slicked back, and his bony complexion suggested a lack of nutrients.

"You know me?" Jeremy asked.

"We all know you. Welcome." The man spoke like a robot. "Would you like to join us?"

"Sure." Jeremy wasn't sure what he was getting into. The two others still hadn't acknowledged him as he pulled up a chair to the table.

The man extended a hand to Jeremy. "Pleasure to meet you. I'm Edgar, everyone just calls me Ed."

"Nice to meet you. Who are your friends?"

"Damon and Dusty. They don't like distractions during puzzle time."

"No, we don't," Damon said without looking up, his black hair hanging like a mop over his chubby face. "Nice to meet you, though. I've heard lots about you." Damon spoke normally, but his refusal to look up from the puzzle rubbed Jeremy the wrong way. But he was in a mental institute, after all—he couldn't expect everyone to have their shit together.

"I got it!" Edgar shouted, holding up a puzzle piece. A grin spread across his serious face. He placed the piece in its correct spot.

Jeremy watched them. "Do you guys work on this puzzle all the time?"

"We try," Ed said. "These guys do the heavy work."

"Don't be modest, Ed, you usually find the one piece we need." Damon clapped his skinny friend on the back.

"What brings you our way after all this time, Jeremy?" Ed

asked.

"Well, I've finally been granted permission to come down here. I've been locked up in my room since Thanksgiving."

"Fascinating," Dusty said. He had a permanent look of curiosity on his face, and his eyes studied everything carefully from behind his glasses.

"How long have you guys been here?" Jeremy asked.

"I've been here seven years," Ed said. His blond hair splayed out in every direction and Jeremy saw craziness behind his muddy eyes.

"Ten years and two hundred thirty one days for me," Damon said.

"Oh, wow, are you counting down or something?" Jeremy asked.

"No, counting up. I've been denied release three times in the last two years. Every year they tell me how much I've improved and how I'm so close, and every year they reject me. Dr. C is full of shit."

Jeremy chuckled, not expecting such honesty from people he just met. "What did you do to get here?"

All three looked at each other before turning back to Jeremy in unison. "That's not something you're supposed to ask," Damon said. "People will tell you once they trust you. But since we all know your story, we might as well share ours. I'm in for robbery. I robbed five banks before being caught. Stole over three million dollars. Didn't even need it, I just enjoy the challenge and the rush."

You're my guy, Jeremy thought. *Smart and ballsy, perfect for an escape partner.*

"I'm anorexic," Dusty said. "The thought of food repulses me." He clenched his stomach.

"I stabbed my mother-in-law," Edgar said with a grin. "I got sick of hearing her opinion about every little thing in my life, and I snapped one day. It's okay, she didn't die, I only stabbed her in the leg."

"Oh, wow." Jeremy wasn't sure what to say to any of them. "Well, here I am. My story is known, it sounds like."

"Fascinating," Dusty said again.

"You're more than welcome to join our group," Edgar said.

"Do you not talk to the others?" Jeremy asked, looking around at the couple dozen people spread across the room.

"Not so much," Dusty said. "We're good friends. The rest of them are assholes. We only talk when we have to at the big events."

"I see," Jeremy said. He didn't want to feel locked in to staying with this group, but they seemed like his kind of people. "How much time do you guys get outside of your rooms?"

"We all have full access to the building. We can do as we please most days," Damon explained. "What is your schedule like?"

"Right now, I'm getting one hour a day until further notice."

"One hour?" Dusty giggled and held his stomach again. Jeremy noticed multiple bandages on his arms.

"Well, have fun with that," Ed said. "Guess you don't have much time then. Would you like to help us with the puzzle?"

Jeremy hated puzzles, but he was willing to suck it up. "Alright."

They returned to the table and the conversation ended, each of them focused on finding the next piece.

11

Chapter 11

Two weeks later, Jeremy had an interview scheduled with a new doctor. This was nothing out of the ordinary, as he had met at least one new doctor each week, in addition to his sessions with Dr. Carpenter.

The nurses always brought a pitcher of lemonade when there was a visiting doctor, and this time was no different. Once the pitcher was delivered, it took less than ten minutes before the young, inexperienced doctor walked through the door with their series of questions ready for the mass murderer. He often wondered if he would've been one of these ambitious psychologists, had he pursued his psychology career instead of slaughtering his coworkers.

He waited at his table, drumming his fingers impatiently for this week's edition of a dipshit shrink. When the doctor entered, Jeremy glanced up and saw an older man with streaks of black hair on an otherwise snowy head that contrasted with his brown skin. Thin-framed glasses perched on the man's big nose, and when Jeremy did a double take of the doctor, his heart froze mid-beat.

"What are you doing here?" Jeremy asked as Dr. Siva

approached the table and sat calmly in the chair. He hadn't seen Dr. Siva since the trial, and hadn't spoken to him in more than two years.

"Good to see you, Jeremy," the doctor said, pouring a glass of lemonade.

"Dr. Siva?" Jeremy didn't know where to begin, as a flood of questions burst through his mind. They hadn't left on bad terms, but Jeremy had blown him off while planning the shooting.

"Yes, Jeremy, it's me. I see you've come a long way since our last talk."

"You could say that." Their last meeting in Dr. Siva's office felt like decades ago. The last time they spoke, Dr. Siva had proposed the idea of getting involved in criminal cases, wanting to make an impact in the courtroom. Jeremy had certainly done that on his own.

He felt like he was dreaming. How was Dr. Siva, his old mentor, sitting across from him in his mental institution room? "Why are you here? How?"

"I'm good friends with Dr. Carpenter. We went to college together and have stayed in touch since. How do you like her?"

"She's good. Treated me well so far."

"And this facility?"

"I've barely been allowed outside of my room over the last couple weeks. The staff is great, though, they make it feel as much like a home as I could ask for."

"Very good. The last time you and I spoke things were a little different. We were talking about how to get mental illness the attention it deserves. I'd say you've accomplished that. I'm very proud of what you've achieved."

Proud? I killed people. I'm not even proud about that, but it had to be done. For the bigger picture.

"Why didn't you ever visit me in jail? Or write me a letter?"

"I wasn't allowed to, then I was subpoenaed as a witness. I followed every bit of news available since I heard about your rampage. I was there every day at the trial, sitting in the back. I was there every step of the way to see what would happen."

Jeremy sat in silence, unsure how to respond.

"I want to ask you a question, Jeremy. It will be kept private. I just need to know for myself."

"Okay?" Jeremy said, still unsure what was actually going on.

"How does it feel knowing you're going to die in this room?"

"Excuse me?"

"I asked how it feels knowing this room is essentially your coffin."

Jeremy scrunched his face in confusion, keeping a steady stare at his old professor. "Why do you say that?" His pulse throbbed, from his toes to his fingertips.

"I say it because it's true. You're never leaving this building, no matter how well you progress. This is your home now."

"That's not what I've been told—"

"I know what you've been told, and I'm telling you it's all a lie. Jeremy, you're a bipolar mass murderer. You'll never see the light of day again."

"Don't call me that." He felt a spark of hot rage, and sat silently, maintaining a glare at his old mentor.

"Jeremy, I've known you were different since the first term paper you wrote for my class. You see, a person reveals a lot about their state of mind through writing. It's one of my specialties, you see. I've done forensic work in examining letters and emails, trying to get inside the head of some seriously dangerous people. I know you planned your attack out. Your mind is too organized to do something on a whim. I never bought the defense's claim that you woke up and decided to kill everyone in your office. I connected the dots. You stopped coming to see me, you ignored my emails, you didn't even enroll in classes for the spring semester. That tells me you were completely consumed by something else. When I saw your face on the news, I knew that was your grand project—what you were working on all that time you were absent."

He actually knows. Jesus Christ.

"Dr. Siva, I didn't plan anything."

"Save it, Jeremy. I knew I could manipulate you into joining me and my experiment. I just didn't think you'd go to such an extreme." Dr. Siva spoke in a condescending voice.

"Manipulate me? You think you made me do this?" Jeremy had to fight the urge to stand up from his chair; if he did, security would have him pinned to the ground in a matter of seconds.

"I didn't *make* you do this, but I planted the seeds. I wanted you to join me in taking down the legal system. That's why I asked you to follow the trial for that young man who shot all the elementary students. I wanted you to see firsthand how a mentally ill person could be so quickly dismissed in a court of law. No consideration was even given to his mental illness."

That's enough of this shit.

"Get the fuck out of my room right now!" Jeremy screamed. "SECURITY!"

Dr. Siva smirked, unfazed by Jeremy's outburst. "No one's coming for you, Jeremy. Dr. Carpenter has called off security for me. She owes me some favors. Now, if you'll let me finish my story."

"Fuck you."

Dr. Siva ignored him. "You had become so checked out as a psychology student, but I knew you were just distracted. I also knew the corporate world would take care of you in time. You were way too brilliant for a regular job; there was never going to be a challenge for you, and you thrive on a good challenge. I thought you had given up at first when I stopped hearing from you, but I knew better. You're not one to just disappear into the night, so I figured you were either distracted by life, or actually doing something useful. I'm so glad things turned out the way they did.

"When I saw you on the news, I didn't waste a second. I knew I had to get you into this facility. I left secret money for your parents and advised them on who to hire as your attorney. I had spent a lot of time in the courtroom and thought of her right away. She's fearless, and exactly what you needed to win that case."

"This is how I know your story is bullshit. It's not that simple. Linda got lucky with the case. She found that dirt on Dr. Reed and made him look like a lying sack of shit."

"Lucky, huh? Who do you think slipped her those files? And yes, Dr. Reed *is* a lying sack of shit."

"So you're just taking credit for everything that went right? Maybe you're the one who should be in here, not me."

"Sure, I did all this not knowing for sure if it would work. An insanity verdict is a long shot regardless of the circumstances. That's why I took one final measure for safety: I threatened the jury forewoman. I went to her house and told her if a guilty verdict came back it was on her life."

"You're a monster," Jeremy said flatly, keeping his rage in check. The last thing he needed was to end up back in a straitjacket.

"And you're bipolar. The sooner you accept it, the better it will be for everyone. We're very excited to get started on studying your mind."

"You went through all this to study my mind?" Jeremy asked, his hands trembling beneath the table. He wanted to lunge across the table and choke Dr. Siva to a painful death.

"We're on the verge of a major breakthrough, Jeremy. A new generation is coming up, much more open-minded than any before. It's our chance to capitalize on this opportunity and show society the truth about mental illness. At a time when people are so focused on human rights, we want to get in on the fun. Add the mentally ill to the ever-growing list of people being stood up for by the next generation."

Jeremy agreed with Dr. Siva—he usually did—but he'd never give him the satisfaction of knowing that.

"I'll never believe this," Jeremy said, more confused than he had ever been. Dr. Siva had to be bluffing; no one could get away with what he had just confessed.

"Why is that? Because you planned it all, right? You lied to yourself, you see. That's how bipolar disorder works. You have two minds, Jeremy, and they don't communicate with each other. I like to think of the disorder as a sort of superpower. There are some spectacular cases of people who mastered the disease and used it to their advantage. You used yours like an evil genius. You're a villain, Jeremy, and you always will be."

"I want you to leave right now."

Jeremy couldn't listen to any more. He could feel his brain boiling, in both disgust and acceptance of what his former professor had to say. He hadn't said anything false, and that was what concerned him.

Maybe he is telling the truth about everything.

Dr. Siva stood calmly. "I'll leave, Jeremy. I'm sure this has been a lot for you to process. But please know I'll be back to study you. I didn't go through all this so you could sit in this room forever. There will be good that comes out of this, you just have to trust me."

"Don't ever show your face here again. I'll make sure you never get the chance to study me."

"You'll change your mind in time. Take your time to get settled. You're still fairly new to the hospital. Take your drugs and trust Dr. Carpenter."

I'm not trusting a goddamn person in this building.

"Good-bye, Jeremy. Till next time." Dr. Siva offered a smile and a nod before turning and leaving the room.

Jeremy stayed in his seat, stunned and mentally drained from the conversation.

There's no way any of that was true. It can't be. I'm here because of me, not because of anything he did.

Jeremy spent the rest of day with his mind stuck in 2015, trying to piece together everything that had happened since his last meeting with Dr. Siva.

12

Chapter 12

Connor waited in darkness, a cool breeze swirling around him. Nighttime had fallen over his new apartment in Pueblo, where he stood outside in the parking lot that separated the complex from the neighboring news station. The gravel crunched below his boots as he paced around the lot to make sure no one was watching him. A row of news vans barricaded the news station from the apartment building, but a path led around the station and toward an open dirt field.

Connor took the path and started to count his steps. Gravel gave way to dirt and he increased his pace. He would be running on this dirt at some point, and he needed to know how it felt beneath his feet.

When he arrived at the perimeter of the Rocky Mountain Mental Health Institute some 2,000 steps later, a sense of excitement took over. A small fence was all that separated him from stepping foot on the campus. He'd expected tighter security for a mental institute, but perhaps it was simply hard to get out of the building. It wasn't a prison, after all.

The main hospital was centered on the campus, surrounded by smaller buildings and open spaces like the soccer field.

Connor navigated around the outermost building to get a clear view of the hospital, where Heston must have been. At night, the building looked more like a hotel, with its five floors of windows stretching from side to side, most of which had the lights turned on. None of the windows had curtains or blinds, leaving Connor a clear view into some of the rooms.

He pulled his binoculars out for a closer look into the rooms, searching window by window for the man he longed to kill. He stayed on the perimeter, not wanting to catch the attention of a wandering security guard.

"Come out, you motherfucker. Where are you?" he whispered under his breath.

About half of the rooms were empty, while others had patients reading books or watching TV.

Connor couldn't see inside any of the fourth or fifth floor windows from his position; he would need to find an elevated position to do so. He started toward the north side of the building, where more patient rooms awaited.

Crickets chirped in the cold silence as the half moon provided just enough light for Connor to not need his flashlight. A group of doctors or nurses, he couldn't tell, walked out the back side of the hospital and crossed toward the building closest to the open field.

The ground returned to pavement as he found himself on a sidewalk running alongside the campus. He walked faster now. The campus covered more ground than he originally thought. He was panting by the time he reached the north side and pulled out his binoculars again.

There was still no one that even resembled Heston in the rooms he could see into.

He's got to be on the upper floors. That's probably where they keep their high-risk patients, trapped in the penthouse to look down at the rest of the world.

He perused for anything he could climb for a higher view and had no luck.

"I'm just gonna walk in." Connor stuffed the binoculars into the small backpack he had brought and started walking on the road that turned into the campus parking lot. The security gate stood at the end of the road, but the parking lot was still accessible, merely separated from the sidewalk by multiple beds of grass running along it. He crossed over the grass and cut through the lot, avoiding the security gate's line of sight.

Though it was past 8 p.m. there were still dozens of cars parked in the lot, and he ducked low as he weaved between them toward the hospital.

When he reached the lot's front row, he stood in clear sight of the hospital. Another bed of grass separated him from the front entrance, where the traffic of people was much heavier than anywhere else. Doctors, nurses, and security guards all paced around the outside of the building, branching off to other areas of the campus. Connor was still dressed in his mud-crusted jeans and flannel shirt that he had worn to the construction site for his day's work.

Fitting in on campus would be impossible, so he decided to stay in the parking lot until he could spot an area with less people.

He crossed the lot, leaving the hospital behind to approach an open space, and strolled up to a different building, where a lone man stood outside smoking a cigarette. He appeared to be a custodian from the looks of his clothes, so Connor stepped onto the sidewalk and walked casually by him. The smoking man made no acknowledgment.

Connor shuffled around the building and stepped foot onto the soccer field. It was a massive open space and he could now see the back of the hospital. A couple of trees stood along the path and he leaned on one to pull out the binoculars and look into the hospital from this new view.

"Goddamn it," he muttered, still unable to find Heston in any of the lower three floors.

He hugged the tree stump and started pulling himself up. The traction on his boots made the climb easier than it should've been. The thickest branch stood roughly eight feet from the ground, but felt much higher once Connor sat on it and looked down.

He scanned the building again, this time able to see into the fourth floor, but not the fifth.

"Holy fucking shit," he whispered. "There you are."

A breeze ruffled the bare tree branches, and through them he saw his target.

Jeremy Heston sat in a room at the end of the building on the fourth floor. He appeared to be reading a book, by the look of his position, although Connor couldn't see for sure what Jeremy was staring down at since his view cut him off at the shoulders.

"Bull's-eye." Connor started to pant again. The sneaking around and climbing had used a lot of energy, but his giddiness made his adrenaline flow. "Easy shot from here," he said, still staring at him through the binoculars.

Connor heard voices from behind him and froze. He'd picked the wrong time of year to hide in a tree, but the voices passed without any questioning. He slid down the stump, brushed off the seat of his pants, and continued exploring the rest of campus.

Now that he knew a clear shot was possible, he needed to plan an escape route. If he fired the shot from the tree, it would be just a matter of minutes before word broke and a search would be underway by the security team. It would need to be a similar night, with low foot traffic. If Jeremy regularly stayed up late into the night, Connor could take his time from the perch in the tree and make sure the shot was lined up perfectly to connect with the murderer's skull.

He also needed to account for the potential of leaves. He had maybe eight more weeks before the leaves would sprout again, making the shot more difficult. With the branches bare, he couldn't hide as well, but the shot was there for the taking.

Away from the hospital, in the opposite direction of the soccer field, Connor found only one other building between himself and the dirt field that led back to his apartment complex. He could see the dim light from his unit in the distance. Behind the building stood a small fence, and Connor approached it to gauge its height.

The top of the chain-link fence stood eye level with him, and he decided his escape route would be to hop this fence and make a dead sprint toward his apartment. Returning to the main road was an obvious bad choice. *The shortest distance between two points is a straight line,* he thought. He hurried back to the tree and counted his paces back to the fence.

About seventy steps. I can sprint that in twenty seconds probably, he thought. He put a foot in the fence and hopped over with ease. His feet hit the dirt with a thud, but the jump was easy. And that was all that mattered.

He eyed the distance to the apartment building and pulled out his phone to set a stopwatch.

"Here goes nothing," he said as he started the timer and

broke into a sprint.

Darkness passed in a blur as the sound of his heavy breathing and pounding boots filled his head. Halfway through the field Connor reached his physical limit. He hadn't run since his high school days and he was paying for it now. That and the constant smoking and drug use that had followed his brother's death.

He imagined his brother's body, in the ground back in Denver, bugs crawling in and out of the various openings of his skeleton. The thought carried him through to the finish line, where he huffed and wheezed in his parking lot. He saw his car and dragged his exhausted legs toward it for something to lean on, and pulled the cell phone out of his pocket.

The sprint had taken fifty seconds. Combine that with the twenty seconds from the tree to the fence, and he had a long minute to shoot Heston and be back in the confines of his apartment.

"No way anyone will catch me in a minute if they don't even know what happened."

He looked at himself in the reflection of the car window and grinned.

13

Chapter 13

Jeremy sat at his table after finishing dinner. He had his copy of *The Shawshank Redemption* pressed open, but stared blankly at the pages. He wasn't going to find a lucky chip in the wall that led to the underground sewers to crawl his way to freedom. That shit only happened in books or movies.

Dr. Siva had sent his mind into a spiral that he hadn't been able to shake for the past couple days. While his old professor's story sounded absurd on the surface, it couldn't be ruled out as a possibility. Everything he claimed to have done could've been realistically achieved. The key turning point (in Jeremy's opinion) in the trial had been the revelation of Dr. Reed's questionable practices and prior testimonies. Dr. Siva knew enough people in the industry that he could have easily bribed or called in a favor for dirt on the prosecution's main witness.

The only part Jeremy had a hard time believing was regarding Dr. Siva threatening a juror. He simply didn't have an intimidating personality, but Jeremy supposed a once in a lifetime opportunity could drive a man to step out of his comfort zone—especially in the name of science.

All along, Dr. Siva had been carrying out the same vision

Jeremy had. *Maybe I should've told him from the start. He probably would've helped me with the planning.*

Jeremy pushed the thoughts out of his mind as best he could. He accepted that he'd likely never know the truth. He requested a phone call with his defense attorney, Linda Kennedy. While she no longer had an obligation to Jeremy, he felt she would be the best place to start with such news. Since Dr. Carpenter had to sign off on all phone requests, Jeremy figured he'd never get to place the call if Dr. Carpenter really was working with Dr. Siva.

I'm fucked. And I'm trapped.

Jeremy decided to regroup and focus on the escape—it was his only possible way out.

He had grown close with his new group of friends in their short time together. They liked to curse and talk in vulgarities, which for him was a return to what felt normal. It reminded him of being in middle school again. They were sincere and genuine, but could he trust his life in their hands?

He had no choice. Every day that passed in the loony bin drove him a bit closer to actual insanity. It didn't help that Dr. Siva had stopped in and planted all sorts of shit in his mind. A knot had been twisting in his gut since his former professor left him dazed by his confession. Perhaps Dr. Siva was already a step ahead of Jeremy and wanted to foil his escape plans. He had said it was his intent to keep him locked up in the hospital forever.

Jeremy tried his hardest to push these thoughts from his mind and focus on an escape. He'd never escape from his room, so would have to milk his time in the commons area for every opportunity.

All you need to do is set yourself up for the opportunity. Jeremy thought back to what his Uncle Ricky used to tell him when they went golfing. *You're not going to make the shot from 150 yards away, but you can put yourself in position for an easy chance on the putt.*

That was all Jeremy could really plan for: the opportunity, the good positioning. He might devise a perfect plan only to see it fail. There were too many moving parts to know how every detail would play out, but if he could just give himself a brief window of chance, he might make it out of the building.

During the free time in the commons area, nurses and guards covered every corner, every patient under constant watch. Because of this, a diversion would be necessary, to draw the attention of all the staff. If a brawl broke out, would a couple of guards try to break it up while the rest of the staff looked on? Not likely, but it would also depend how the other patients reacted. If they tried to join in on the fun, then he'd have his chance, with the entire staff consumed. If they sat back and watched, the diversion did him no good.

Should he succeed in causing a playground-type brawl, slipping out the front door might be an option, depending on the receptionist. She wouldn't have a chance at stopping him, especially from behind her desk. But she could shout for a guard if she saw him trying to exit. Perhaps he could clock her in the head and walk out like a champ. It all depended on the severity of the diversion.

He needed more time to study the layout of the hospital's main floor. The front entrance was the only door he had seen that led to the outside world. There was a courtyard for the patients to use, but it appeared to be enclosed by the building. Maybe one of his friends would have more knowledge about potential exits.

Dr. Carpenter had avoided Jeremy since Dr. Siva's visit, probably knowing he would be angry about what he had said. She'd relayed through the nurses that his free time in the commons was increased to two hours each day.

She also granted him a notebook, which Jeremy left untouched on his table. The thought of devising another plan in one made him sick that he been tricked into doing it the first time around. The lonely nights plotting every detail of the shooting felt like ages ago. Besides, anything he wrote in a notebook could easily be picked up by a doctor or nurse to be reviewed.

He stared out his window to the darkness swallowing the campus. The few lights that twinkled in the distance always gave him hope. There was still a world out there, and he intended to be a part of it.

14

Chapter 14

The final day of January arrived and Connor couldn't take it anymore. Ever since he'd seen Heston in his room, living a peaceful life, the urge to take that life had grown stronger by the hour. It reached a point where he had to acknowledge that the entire situation was starting to affect his life. His mind ran on autopilot; he needed drugs to help him sleep, and more drugs to help him focus during the day. The carousel of alcohol, cocaine, and marijuana took their toll on his already fading body. If he kept it up any longer he'd have no chance of completing the sprint from the campus to his apartment.

"You're dead tonight," he said when he arrived home, staring out his window at the hospital. The workday had worn him out, so he snorted a line of coke to keep his mind sharp and provide a false sense of energy. He inhaled deeply, letting the drug fill his body. His confidence surged through the roof in mere seconds.

He snatched the rifle from his closet, confirmed the lone round in the chamber, and lay down on his sleeping bag with the gun clenched in his embrace. He intentionally loaded only one round, not wanting the temptation to keep shooting should he miss. One shot was all he needed; he had full confidence in his aim, especially with the coke to help him.

He pulled his phone out and saw that it was 5:30. Nine o'clock was his target time. The campus would be deserted and Jeremy would be in his room, hopefully sitting at the table as he had done the two other times Connor spied on him during the past month.

Connor kept an old CD player with him and popped in an old Eminem CD to help him get in the right frame of mind. His stomach growled, but he wasn't sure if it was hunger or nerves. The thought of finally killing Heston excited him, but the sprint back to the apartment weighed heavily on his mind. A lot could go wrong. Even though he had practiced, it had been without a gunshot sending him off to the races. Tonight would be different, but he wished for more of the same.

He considered getting in his car and driving off, instead of running to the apartment. He could get to Colorado Springs in a few minutes and hang out at a bar to wait for the news to break. Or maybe the smarter choice was to drive back to Denver and ditch the rifle at his apartment. The odds of him being questioned by police were unlikely, at least so soon. It would be wise to completely get rid of the gun. No gun to tie it to him, a spent bullet the only trace of evidence if found.

Forensics might eventually figure it out, but how hard would they honestly try to figure out the death of that scumbag piece of shit? Hopefully people would consider it a courageous act. Certainly the family members of the deceased would. Taking the law into your own hands was usually frowned upon, but this was a clear exception to the rule.

Insanity, my ass. This country will only go further down the shitter if we start letting these pussy millennials get away with cold-blooded murder.

"Eye for an eye. If I could kill you thirteen times, I would."

Connor spent the next hour trying to clear his mind. He knew what he had to do—no point in overexciting himself. Instead, he tried to imagine the news stories that would break later that night. All the vans that waited outside his apartment would make the short drive to the institute. Reporters would stand in front of the hospital, possibly even in the back, where a shattered window would appear above.

"Just behind me, someone has fired a shot into the room of Jeremy Heston, the mass murderer who killed thirteen of his coworkers two years ago," Connor said in his best newscaster impression. Doctors would be interviewed, along with anyone who happened to be on campus at the time.

He closed his eyes and pictured what he wanted: the headline "JEREMY HESTON DEAD!" Only then would life feel right again.

"I can do this."

The hour passed more quickly than he'd expected. Thanks to the drugs, his sense of time was off. He snorted more coke, the high already wearing off.

"Two more hours, Heston. Enjoy the last minutes of your cock-sucking life."

He paced around the apartment for the next hour, stopping for an occasional glance out the window, to see the hospital begging him to bring justice to its phony patient.

* * *

When 8:30 arrived, Connor snorted one more line of powder

and zipped up his jacket. A snow storm was predicted to pound the area around midnight, dropping temperatures to the low twenties.

He stepped into the parking lot and walked to his car, which he had moved to the edge closest to where he would be returning from the campus. He decided, right then, to leave town after all. His rifle hung on a strap over his shoulder, and he kept it tucked away under his arm as best he could. The sight of a man dressed in all black toting a long-distance rifle would surely grab attention, but the darkness would help to cover him.

He trudged into the dirt field, checking over his shoulder a couple times to make sure no one from the news station was watching. With the coast clear, he picked up his pace once he reached the sidewalk that wrapped around to the institute's main entrance. The night was too cold for any crickets, leaving only the sounds of his breathing and his clicking boots to echo in the silence.

Adrenaline started to flush its way through his veins, and it combined with the cocaine to make his heart feel like it might burst through his chest. His breathing grew heavy and he could see it leave his mouth in frozen clouds.

He turned the corner into the entrance and found nothing out of the ordinary. The grass beds were crunchier and slicker than usual, thanks to the frosty dew starting to form, but it was nothing to worry about.

There was less traffic than normal in the hospital's main lobby. The campus also remained deserted. He could see people walking in the distance, but there was not a soul in the area between the soccer field and his special tree.

He crossed the soccer field, conscious of his pace so as not to appear out of place. He strolled across the grass like it was a Saturday afternoon at the park, only with his rifle resting carefully along his side.

The tree waited for him, leafless and ready for him to perch on its biggest branch. As he approached it he could see the light in Heston's room and his heart thumped wildly again.

He climbed the tree, its frozen bark scraping his chest and belly as his arms wrapped around the stump. *Should've worn gloves,* he thought when he saw the small streaks of blood on his fingers when he reached his perch. He saddled the branch and rocked back and forth to ensure he was properly balanced. Falling out of the tree because of the gun's backfire would throw a major wrench into the escape plan.

With his position secured, he slid the rifle off his shoulder and raised it to look through the scope. Heston's head appeared in the same position as it had a couple weeks prior. He was a creature of habit, and for that Connor was grateful. The coast remained clear. He was free to take his time and line up the perfect shot.

"Time to punch your ticket to hell," Connor whispered. His heart continued to pound like a caged, rabid animal. The feeling spread to his fingertips as they throbbed uncontrollably on the rifle. His vision also pulsed in and out of focus, zeroing in on the piece of shit behind the window.

Heston appeared to be sitting stiffly and upright, as if he were looking straight ahead at something. Possibly a TV on the wall? What would be the last thing that murdering son of a bitch would see before his lights went out?

"Who gives a fuck. Enjoy the blackness."

Connor slid his finger over the trigger as he moved a steady hand to align the crosshairs perfectly on the back of Jeremy's head.

15

Chapter 15

Jeremy sat at his table like any other night, making his best effort to stay awake. If he sat on his couch or bed it always led to him tipping over and calling it a night. And why should he sleep when there was so much planning to do?

He had a stack of books now at his disposal, but he kept them piled in a neat stack at the edge of the table. Reading made him sleepy and he liked to save that for right before bedtime.

Instead, he let his mind wander about the escape. He believed he had figured out a way to cause the brawl he needed, but still wanted to run it by his friends. While he wouldn't hang back to help them, he planned to incentivize them with the opportunity to escape once the brawl broke loose. It would be every man for themselves at that point, and if they could make it out, more power to them.

His plan was to play off of each patient's weakness. He didn't know what everyone had been hospitalized for, but surely his friends would have that information. To his knowledge, there were anorexics, bulimics, alcoholics, thieves, violent offenders, and gambling addicts.

The most difficult—likely impossible—ones to rattle would

be the alcoholics. There was certainly no alcohol he could get his hands on anywhere on campus, to try and tempt them to jump off the wagon. The anorexics and bulimics could be bribed with food. He could get into a discussion with them and start cramming all available snacks down his gullet while they watched. Once he had their attention he would start throwing the food at them, maybe even force it down their throats. For the thieves, surely it would upset them to fall victim to their own favorite crime. They could pick fights with the violent offenders, and invite the gambling addicts to the card games that always seemed to be taking place. Since there was never money involved, Jeremy could up the stakes with friendly wagers. He knew bragging rights were just as big a part of gambling as winning money.

He stared at the wall as he imagined the actual escape after the diversion. The front door would be a drastic and unlikely option. Instead, he could slip through the door that led to the courtyard and hop the fence that kept it separated from the rest of the campus. From there it would be a foot race to freedom. He'd need to locate the main road and run in the opposite direction, away from the road. His campus knowledge was limited to the view from his window, which faced the long stretch of never-ending campus toward the mountains. Would anyone have the courage to pick up a hitchhiker in a city that housed both mental health patients and prisoners?

His best hope was to find his way into the neighborhood that separated the campus from the interstate and find somewhere to hide. He couldn't know how intense of a search would be set out for him. Bloodhounds would possibly be deployed to track him down, knowing he couldn't get too far on foot.

He longed for the moment when he'd be making a run for

it, chasing his dream of exposing mental health. He wanted to write the book about his treatment in jail as a mentally ill convict awaiting trial for two years. All the experience at the institute provided plenty of bonus material, too.

His brain itched with fatigue, but he wanted to fight through it and stay up another hour. If he could catch a second wind, he knew his best thoughts would come then.

Suddenly, his window exploded, shards of glass bursting across the room. Jeremy jumped out of his chair and grabbed the back of his right shoulder, a burning sensation filling his arm from shoulder to elbow.

"Motherfuck!" he barked. "What the fuck!"

He removed his hand from his shoulder and saw fresh blood coating his fingers. Warm liquid trickled from his shoulder down the rest of his arm, and the room started to spin around him. The shattered window let in a rush of freezing air, but he couldn't feel it, his body slowly turning numb throughout.

Jeremy's legs gave way as he slid down the wall and curled into a fetal position on the floor, blood pooling beneath his shoulder as he fell into unconsciousness.

16

Chapter 16

By the time Jeremy woke up in St. Luke's Medical Center an hour later, Connor was halfway to Denver, coasting down I-25 at the speed limit, to not draw any attention to himself. He flipped through the radio stations, impatiently waiting to hear the breaking news coming out of Pueblo. There hadn't been a peep yet about what had happened. Why was the story taking so long to break?

He checked his cell phone, but all that was reported from the *Pueblo Daily News* was that there had been an incident at the mental institute. They didn't even mention a shooting, or the death of their infamous patient. The world would rejoice at Heston's death, so why not break the good news?

He didn't stick around to see the outcome, but was confident he had hit Heston in the head, based on the way his head had flung back. The escape route went smoother than anticipated. The shot echoed around the campus, but he could have probably walked out the front entrance without anyone noticing.

By the time he reached his car a minute later, he looked back to the campus and found there was still no one outside looking for him. He put his rifle in his trunk, jumped into the driver's seat, and left his apartment behind.

"Remember, they can't search your car without a warrant," he told himself, preparing for a potential roadside stop from the police. "If they ask where you're going, just say you want to take a long weekend back home."

Connor felt the fear of being caught take control of his mind. Why should he have to go through the legal system and face punishment for killing an actual monster? He was doing the world a favor. The victims' families would want to give him a medal for getting revenge on the man who had ruined their lives.

When he arrived back in Denver, there had still been no news on the radio. How long did it take for these stories to become public? His cell phone rang. It was his mom calling.

"Connor, where are you?" Her voice trembled.

"Hi, Mom. I'm home. At my apartment in Denver. Why, what's going on?"

"Thank God. We were watching the news and they said there was a shooting at the mental institute in Pueblo. Someone shot Jeremy Heston in his room!"

About time. Connor grinned in relief, then had to fake a surprised reaction.

"You're kidding me! Is he dead?" He awaited the sweet response he'd been longing to hear for years.

"No." Connor's heart sunk. "They're saying he was shot and wounded, was taken to the hospital, and is being treated there. The cops are still looking for the shooter."

"And you thought it was me?"

"Of course not!"

"Then why did you act so relieved that I was here?"

His mom paused for a few seconds.

"I didn't think anything at first. I was excited, to tell you the truth. But then I kept thinking about it, and you living in Pueblo right now.... I just know how much you hate him, I wanted to make sure you didn't do something you'd regret."

"Well, I didn't." *I only regret that it didn't kill him.*

"Okay then. I'm glad you're okay."

"Tell me, Mom, do you want him to die?"

"Of course I do," she said without hesitation.

"Okay. Well, let's hope it goes downhill for him at the hospital. I'll call you later."

Connor hung up and immediately started pacing around his apartment.

"How the fuck didn't he die? I shot him in the head!" Rage boiled up in him. He'd had one chance to take Heston out of the world, and it looked like he had failed. Security would be tightened at the hospital by tomorrow, and there would certainly be no more strolling through the front entrance with a long-range rifle ever again.

He turned on his TV. The news finally flooded the networks, Heston's mugshot appearing on every channel. Footage from Pueblo's own KWGA Network, his neighbor, showed a young reporter standing in front of the hospital's main entrance. Red and blue lights flashed like strobe lights in the background as groups of police officers huddled around.

"Investigators are still trying to piece together this puzzle," the reporter said. "There are only a couple of locations where they believe a gunman would have had a clear shot to hit Mr. Heston, based on his position in his room."

He wanted an update on Heston, so he kept flipping the channels, stopping when he saw a reporter speaking outside the medical hospital in Pueblo. The young blond spoke in front

81

of the emergency room entrance.

"Word from inside the hospital is that Jeremy Heston is in stable condition. The bullet was lodged in his shoulder, and investigators look forward to swabbing it for fingerprints. There's no word yet on when he will be released from the hospital, to return to the mental institute. His family has not returned our inquiries for comment."

Stable condition. Bullet in the shoulder? How did this all go so wrong?

He sat down on his couch, a luxury he missed since moving to his studio in Pueblo, and felt his stomach sink into his legs. He'd loaded the round with gloves on, anticipating a potential fingerprint search, but the thought of investigators having it in their possession put him on edge.

Detectives would likely contact him at some point, not necessarily out of suspicion, but rather due diligence. After all, he was related to one of Heston's victims, and he lived in Pueblo.

"I need to drive back tonight," he said into his empty apartment. He started to sweat, not sure if it was nerves or withdrawal. He had left in such a rush that he didn't grab coke, weed, or anything to calm himself. It was all at his apartment in Pueblo.

He hadn't taken time off work, and calling in at this point would put a bull's-eye on his back as soon as investigators looked into his whereabouts. Work would be miserable, but he'd have to suck it up and make it through the rest of the week. Maybe then he would come back for the weekend in Denver, to get away from the drama and let things die down.

Chapter 17

Jeremy couldn't remember the ride to the hospital. The last thing he could recall was staring out the shattered window after he collapsed to the floor. The stars had glowed magically as he drifted into unconsciousness.

The paramedics had arrived within ten minutes after the slug caught him in the shoulder. A nurse was making her rounds on the fourth floor, heard the shatter of glass, and immediately called security. Security checked the cameras on the floor and saw Jeremy lying limp in his room, beneath the window.

Dr. Carpenter was called in after hours as the night turned to complete chaos. Officers and detectives crawled around the campus in search of clues. The security team worked closely with them and provided surveillance footage that covered every inch of the campus.

When Jeremy woke in a hospital room (a regular hospital!), he could recollect everything that had happened in his room and recount the story to the police officer waiting for him to wake up.

"I was in my room meditating, like every night," he told him. "My window exploded and I felt a numbing pain in my arm. I had no idea I was shot, tried to stand up to see what was going on, and then it all went black."

"Has anyone made threats against you?" the police officer asked him. He was noticeably nicer to Jeremy than any of the ones back in Denver had been.

"No. Just the opposite, actually—I've made friends at the institute, and we're getting along quite well."

So this is the shock that comes with being shot. Jeremy couldn't help but acknowledge the dreamlike sense that had taken hold of his mind—an out-of-body experience.

A doctor entered the room and politely asked the officer to step outside for a few minutes.

"Hi, Jeremy, I'm Dr. Blanchard." The older man stuck out a hand that Jeremy shook weakly. "How are you feeling?"

"Okay, I guess. A little loopy, but I can remember everything that happened except for coming here."

"Very good." The doctor had a head full of thick gray hair and a pair of crooked glasses resting on the bridge of his nose. "You lost a lot of blood. The bullet came very close to your subclavian artery. Another half-inch and it would have ruptured it, and you wouldn't be here. Consider yourself lucky."

I've been lucky all along. I should have been a human shooting target two years ago.

"You may be here a couple days. We've replaced your blood and need to make sure it stabilizes in your system. Other than that, you'll only have lingering pain in the shoulder."

Jeremy nodded. The thought of being half an inch from death made him queasy. Death wasn't supposed to arrive so soon. He still had a mission to fulfill, and his mind was finally back to fully functioning, thanks to his secret disposal of the medication given at the institute.

"Do I get to watch TV here?" Jeremy asked, nodding to the small TV across the room. He couldn't remember the last time he had laid in bed and watched TV.

"Of course, the remote is on your right, feel free to help yourself. If you need anything else, just page a nurse. Did you have questions for me regarding your shoulder?"

"I don't believe so. Am I drugged up right now? Because I don't feel anything."

"Yes. You're on morphine. We'll lower the dosage over the next couple days so you can be ready to get out of here."

That explains the numb body and my giddiness.

"Is everyone at the institute okay?"

"I believe so. No one else was brought in, but I'm sure Officer Torres will be able to answer that better."

Dr. Blanchard let him know he'd be back to check on him later and left him to his TV. Officer Torres let himself back in.

"Hi, Officer, was anyone else injured tonight?" Jeremy asked him, hoping to guide the conversation. Even though he was the victim this time around, being alone with a cop still made him uneasy.

"No, it was a targeted attack. We've discovered security footage. It's blurry, but clear that a man with a rifle walked onto the campus, posted up in a tree outside your window, pulled the trigger, and made a run for it. He disappeared into a field out of reach of the cameras, so he's still on the loose. We're checking around the neighborhood and also with the news station in town. He may have run toward their building, so if they have any footage, we might be able to piece more of this together."

"I don't understand how he was able to get so close."

"Security is good on campus; however, it's designed to keep

patients from getting out rather than to keep people from entering. He walked onto the grounds fairly easy without being seen, especially at such a late hour. Dr. Carpenter has called for an entire revamp of campus security."

"Oh, good." Jeremy started to giggle out of his control. "Sorry, Officer, I think it's the painkiller."

Officer Torres couldn't help but grin, but didn't say anything in response. "We've already launched an investigation. We're going to start by interviewing survivors and victims' relatives from your shooting two years ago."

"Will I be safe here?"

"Yes, there will be an officer or hospital security outside your room during your entire stay."

"Great." Jeremy immediately started to try to figure out a way to escape the hospital; it would certainly be easier than escaping from the institute, since it was unlikely to be guarded.

"I'll let you get back to resting, but I'll be in touch with any updates." Officer Torres gave a warm smile.

"Thanks, Officer."

The cop left the room and Jeremy tried to get his bearings. The white board on the wall below the TV showed his room number as 237; he assumed that meant he was on the second floor. A look out his window showed a view of open fields, suggesting that he was facing the east side of Pueblo.

He looked down and saw that his body had been draped with a thin hospital gown. He pulled up the collar and saw his naked self beneath.

If he were to be guarded during his stay in the hospital, then there was no way out. He could only hope his protector would take a lap around the hall at some point and allow him to make a run for it. Anything was possible.

Jeremy wondered who the hell had shot him.

Has to be a survivor of the shooting, he thought. And that meant it was one of his former coworkers. *Who that survived would have access to a gun, and know how to use it so well?*

He thought of Clark. Clark had a gun, but was never an angry or vengeful person. It was possible the survivor's guilt could have changed him, but Jeremy thought it unlikely.

Clark would rather come talk to me than shoot me.

The cop had said they were investigating family members of his victims. That opened the door to endless possibilities. It could have been someone passing through Pueblo, wanting to take a shot at becoming a hero. He wasn't oblivious to the fact that there were probably hundreds, if not thousands, who desperately wanted him dead.

Jeremy started to doze, and fought to keep his eyes open. The morphine was too strong, though, and he fell into a deep sleep until the next morning, dreaming of a way to escape.

* * *

Arlene Heston powered down her laptop and sat in the dark office of her new home in Flagstaff. After learning of Jeremy being shot, her first instinct had been to pack a suitcase and board the next plane to Denver. She was only halfway finished filling her suitcase when Robert appeared in their bedroom doorway, tipsy, holding three shoe boxes stacked on each other.

"What are those?" she asked, continuing to throw clothes into the suitcase.

"These are why I don't want you to go anywhere near

Colorado," he said flatly. "These are why we moved. I was hoping to never have to share these with you, but I suppose now I should, before you decide to head for the airport."

Robert had made it clear that he would never visit Jeremy, saying that their son was "already dead" as far as he was concerned. She resented him for it, hated him a little bit, in fact, but she recognized that her own emotions had been on a nonstop roller coaster since Jeremy's massacre in 2016.

We all deal with tragedy differently. Just because he's my husband doesn't make him exempt from that fact, she reminded herself daily, during her constant thoughts of returning to Colorado for a brief stint.

Part of the reason she hadn't left yet was a fear of encountering Jeremy alone. What if he was stoned off his ass from the medications they gave him? What if he was locked in a private cell with a muzzle over his face like Hannibal Lecter? The possibilities made her nauseous.

"Are you going to show me what's in the boxes?" she asked after Robert had remained frozen in the doorway.

"Yes. Just remember, I kept this all from you for your own good. You were already in bad shape after the shooting, I didn't want this to send you into a tailspin."

Robert shuffled to the foot of their bed, nudged Arlene's suitcase to create space, and dropped the stack of shoe boxes on the bed.

"These boxes have all the letters sent to us," Robert said, flipping the lid open on the top box.

"Letters from who?" Arlene asked, joining her husband at his side.

"I suppose you could call it fan mail and death threats. Have a look for yourself."

Arlene reached into the box with a shaky hand and grabbed the top letter, a folded sheet of loose leaf paper. She spread it open and read.

DIE HESTONS DIE! was scribbled in furious handwriting.

Arlene felt her heart sink at the sight of the note. She folded it back up and exchanged it for another note.

LEAVE DENVER OR WE'LL BURN YOUR HOUSE DOWN WHILE YOU SLEEP! read another note.

MENTAL ILLNESS IS NOT AN EXCUSE FOR MURDER. GOD WILL DAMN YOUR FAMILY INTO HELL FOREVER.

IF JEREMY LIVES, YOU WILL DIE!

"How many are there?" Arlene asked, her arms trembling as she studied the stack of shoe boxes.

"Hundreds," Robert said, staring at them as well. "Possibly thousands, I haven't counted them. I informed the police when they started coming to our house, but they said not to worry about it. Apparently this is common for relatives of mass murderers. It's why I was in such a hurry to get us moved out of Denver. Even if one of these threats is real, why take the chance?"

Tears streamed down Arlene's face as she sat on the bed and buried her face in her palms.

"When did this all start?" she asked, voice muffled.

"The week after his shooting they started coming in. Then they fizzled out until the trial started again, then we started getting a mailbox full of them every day. No one ever leaves a return address, but from the postmarks they came from all around the country."

"I wish you would've told me about these sooner."

"I wish I never had to tell you about it. But do you see why it's not safe to go back?"

"I still don't think there will be any harm. How will anyone know that I'm back in town unless I announce it?"

"We're still being followed and tracked, Arlene," Robert said, shaking his head. "We've gotten a few letters at this new address."

"What?" she asked, jumping off the bed. "What do you mean? Have you seen anyone?"

Robert shrugged. "I've seen people walking by sometimes and they stare at the house, but don't stop. I don't know if it's my paranoid mind or just nosy people."

"What are we going to do?" Arlene demanded. "How am I supposed to sleep at night now?"

Robert chuckled, the aroma of scotch oozing from his lips. "Why do you think I drink every day? It's the only way to sleep and stay relaxed. I've looked at some houses in Canada and Mexico—it might be best for us to just leave the country and start over somewhere else."

Arlene crossed her arms and paced in circles around their bedroom. She wouldn't say that she hated her life since the shooting, but joy sure came at a premium now. And just when she felt her life was settling back into a somewhat normal groove, Robert dropped this new information on her.

It explained so much, including his binge drinking. He had been living with this heavy secret for years now, and had to continue every day like everything was fine. He was right, too. She wouldn't have been able to handle multiple death threats every day, especially in the months following the shooting when she barely left the bedroom. She would've certainly spiraled into a depression that might not have had an end in sight.

Nothing would ever be normal again, not after Jeremy killed

all of those innocent people.

With Jeremy now under a mental asylum's care—and currently in a medical hospital from a bullet wound he undoubtedly deserved—Arlene finally saw things from Robert's perspective.

Jeremy had said nothing to explain himself when they had visited him in jail before the trial. He ignored them, refused eye contact throughout the entire trial. Even a quick glance from her Jer-Bear would've been a token of faith that he was still alive somewhere inside his damaged and demented mind.

But none of that happened.

Their kind and caring son was gone. His soul had vanished and was replaced by a psychotic killing monster. Arlene had known this deep down, but never accepted it until she saw the boxes filled with hate mail. Her son had flipped the world on its axis and ruined many more lives than she had initially realized. How many people out there were just as angry, but never took the time to write and mail a letter?

Visiting Jeremy would do nothing to put her mind at ease; she had no connection to whatever soul now loomed behind his facade. There would be no closure. Jeremy had already checked out of this world.

She turned to her husband, dark pits below his eyes and sagging skin from days of constant stress. "What do you think about Europe instead?"

18

Chapter 18

Connor sat in the Pueblo Police Department's main lobby, his leg bouncing uncontrollably as his palms turned clammy. He had received a phone call at six in the morning from a man who identified himself as Detective Calkins.

The detective said that Connor was a person of interest in the shooting of Jeremy Heston and asked if he wouldn't mind coming down to the precinct for questioning. Connor felt his heart rummage around in his chest before it sunk into his gut.

"Yeah, I can stop in. Should I call in sick? My work starts at eight." He tried his best to sound normal, but his own ears couldn't recognize his high-pitched voice.

"You'll want to tell them you're coming in later in the morning," the detective said sternly.

As Connor waited, he tried to clear his mind from the fact that he had shot Heston. In fact, he tried to clear the very existence of Heston from his memory. Police officers passed him by, ignoring him, and he wondered if one of them might be keeping an eye on him, to see his current mood. He fought to settle his nerves.

"Mr. Chappell?" a man in a suit and tie asked as he approached from around the corner.

"Yes, sir." Connor's voice came out clear and concise. *Keep that up.*

"Thank you for coming in. I'm Detective Calkins." The detective, a man in his early thirties by the looks of his perfect skin and full head of thick black hair, extended a strong handshake. "Let's head back so I can ask you some questions in private. Follow me."

Connor followed the detective down a short hallway, passing a handful of closed doors. His heart started to pound again.

The detective turned a corner and walked into his office. A cluttered desk with multiple files spread about was centered in the small room. Outside the window Connor could see the station's parking lot.

Detective Calkins sat down in his chair, which squeaked with every movement he made. Connor sat across from him, relieved not to be in an actual interrogation room.

The detective opened a file and thumbed through the pages. "Alright, Mr. Chappell. Just so you know, you're a person of interest in this case."

"Why is that?" Connor's voice cracked.

"Well, your brother was murdered by Jeremy Heston in the Denver office shooting. Mr. Heston was located at the Rocky Mountain Mental Health Institute, which is less than a half mile from your new apartment. For obvious reasons, you stand out compared to other victims' relatives."

"Okay, that's understandable."

"Why did you get an apartment here in Pueblo recently?"

"I got assigned a project from January through the summer. I work in construction for the Phelps Brothers."

"And what's the status of your residence in Denver?"

"It's empty. I live by myself. I try to check on it every couple weekends or so."

The detective was scribbling notes on a large pad of paper.

"Were you aware that Jeremy Heston was at the mental health institute near your apartment?"

"I knew he was in Pueblo, so I figured that was probably the spot. I haven't had much of a chance to explore the area. Sundays have been my only day off, for the most part."

"Do you own any guns?"

"Yes, I have a Glock 35." He did have one at his Denver apartment. He also had his rifle, which kept trying to creep into his mind. It had been gifted to him by his father and was not on the records as belonging to him personally.

"Any access to a rifle?"

Connor scrunched his face in thought. "Not that I know of. My family has always been big into pistols."

"Is there anyone in your family that might have been involved in this shooting?"

"No. It's just my parents that are left, and they never leave the house anymore."

"Where were you last night between seven and ten?"

"Denver." Connor said it as fast as he could. Any moment's hesitation could cost him everything. Let the detective ask more questions if he needed.

The detective raised his eyebrows, creating wrinkles on his forehead. "Denver? On a weeknight? What was the occasion?"

"I had to grab some things. I've only been living down here a month and am basically living out of my suitcase. I don't even have a bed or any furniture."

"What things did you need to get that required a four-hour round trip?"

Fuck.

"Some clothes...books...and the last of my snacks. Didn't want them to go bad."

"Of course not."

Detective Calkins stayed silent as he flipped through more pages in his file, and it drove Connor to near insanity.

"Alright, Mr. Chappell. You're free to go. I'll be in touch, be sure to stay in town."

"Yes, sir. Thank you." Connor stood and the detective extended a hand.

"Thanks for coming in and cooperating." Connor shook his hand with his own trembling hand.

The detective remained standing with his arms crossed as Connor walked out of his office.

Chapter 19

The hospital discharged Jeremy on the evening of February 2, sending him back to the mental institute. A guard had remained on duty the entire time he was in the hospital, leaving him no chance of an escape.

Of course it couldn't be that easy, he thought.

Jeremy returned to his same room, where the window had been replaced with a bulletproof pane of glass. Apparently he would be staying in the room for an extended period of time, if they felt the need to permanently secure the window.

Dr. Carpenter was already sitting at the table when he entered, no paperwork with her this time.

"Jeremy, how are you doing?"

"Okay, I guess. Aside from knowing I almost died."

Jeremy actually felt completely fine. Sure, he'd had a scare, but he felt a laser focus that had been missing since his initial days of planning his massacre. He couldn't tell this to Dr. Carpenter; he had to show normal human emotion.

"I'm sure. I've been in contact with your doctors at the hospital, and once they assured me you were going to be fine, I focused on increasing security here on campus. We've never had anything like this happen, so a lot of research had to be done quickly to make sure proper measures were put into place."

"Are you sure I'm safe in here? What's changed?" Jeremy wanted to know how these changes might affect his escape plans.

"Seeing as this shooter walked onto campus without a problem, construction is beginning tomorrow at the main entrance, to build walls around the perimeter. This will ensure that everyone has to go through the security check-in. More cameras are being installed, and we'll have hourly sweeps of the campus done by the security team."

"What procedures are currently in place?" Jeremy faked frustration, wanting to ruffle Dr. Carpenter and hopefully get her to reveal valuable information he could use later.

"You have to understand, we're essentially in the middle of nowhere. After talking with our security team, they don't recall ever having pedestrian traffic come onto campus. The only place that's walking distance from here is the surrounding neighborhood, and possibly the mall if someone wanted a long walk. We're nothing but a hospital, keep in mind. Our security was on par with the expectations for most medical centers around the country. We have the footage of the man who did this, they just haven't been able to make out a clear profile."

So there's a neighborhood nearby. And a mall. A mall won't do me any good, but a neighborhood I can work with. Lots of places to hide in a neighborhood.

Jeremy thought back to his childhood days, when he and the neighborhood kids would gather and play hide-and-seek. He always took pride in finding the most impossible places to squeeze into and stay out of sight for long stretches of time.

"Who pays for my hospital bills?" Jeremy had sort of hoped his parents would be sent a bill; maybe then they would try to get in contact with him.

"We have an insurance policy that covers any incident occurring within the institute. So it's all covered."

"Have my parents been notified?"

"We have reached out, but have not connected with them."

Jeremy sat back in his chair and rubbed his eyes. Even though the morphine had kept him knocked out for most of the stay in the hospital, he still felt exhausted. Perhaps it was still working its way out of his system.

"Am I able to get in touch with them?" he asked.

"We can arrange for a call to them. I'll have my team reach out to see when they may be available. But keep in mind, Jeremy, we have made attempts and invited them to visit with no response."

"Thank you." He ignored her comment, knowing they would come visit if he asked directly.

"Jeremy," Dr. Carpenter said. "You need to face the fact that you might not hear from your parents again. It happens more than you might think. When a family member is admitted to a mental hospital, it can affect the relatives in unpredictable ways."

"Thank you, Doctor. I know my parents, and if I can speak to them, they'll listen."

Dr. Carpenter sighed. "In the meantime, I'll be checking in with you more frequently. You were progressing tremendously and I want to make sure this event doesn't cause any setbacks."

"I'm fine. I swear."

"That's great. I'll still be checking in. Trauma can have subtle and sometimes unseen effects."

Trauma? I killed thirteen of my coworkers in cold blood, and she thinks I'm *suffering from trauma?*

"Okay. Fair enough. Will you be continuing my pain medication, or is that through another doctor?"

"That will be another doctor. They've provided us with pain meds to give you for the next week. A doctor will be in to see you when the week is up, to decide if you need to continue."

She let him know the plan for the next week and then left him to try and return to his usual routine.

20

Chapter 20

Linda Kennedy debated visiting Jeremy to see how her infamous client was holding up in the mental hospital. Since the trial had ended, life hadn't returned to normal for the superstar attorney. As her colleague and mentor, Wilbert, had predicted before she accepted the case, she found herself with a constant influx of customers virtually lining up out the door.

She had to check her voicemails twice a day, each time clearing out at least ten inquiries for her services. The success was a win for her entire firm, as she had no possible way of handling all the dozens of cases they accepted each month.

To handle the inquiries, the firm promised its clients that Linda would consult on the case, but not be able to offer her services in the courtroom due to scheduling restrictions. Wilbert had proposed this as a temporary solution until things died down, but coming up on three months with no end in sight, she started to wonder when she could get back to what she regarded as normal work: working with a handful of clients each month and seeing their cases through from beginning to end.

Ever since Judge Zamora read the verdict on that fateful day in November, Linda had been stretched to the moon and back. The first month saw hundreds of media requests for interviews and TV appearances. Even late-night talk show hosts requested her presence, which she accepted without a second thought. Free flights and hotels in New York lured her away from her job, but Wilbert had forced her to take thirty days to recover from the grueling trial, so why not take advantage of the downtime?

She thought back to those hectic two weeks of being in a different city every night. Her mind had grown numb to answering the same questions about defending the infamous, insane mass murderer.

No, they didn't speak much. No, Jeremy never made a confession about why he carried out the shootings. No, she didn't think all murderers should be set free based on her case's outcome.

Her interviewers should have already known the answers, but they asked anyway, hungry for their own special on the most controversial court case since O.J. Simpson. She knew her window of opportunity would be short-lived and she had to take advantage before the media moved on to the next person of interest. Or the next mass shooting.

When the voicemail light blinked endlessly on her office phone, she couldn't help but wonder if it was a mistake going on her brief publicity tour. Would life be somewhat normal if she had just disappeared to a beach in Mexico and drunk margaritas for a month?

Lately, she couldn't help but get the image of Jeremy out of her mind. Him standing beside her in court, hearing the judge read his not guilty by reason of insanity verdict, the crowd behind them losing their minds as a result. Him turning to her after the twenty minutes of verdict readings, a look of shock on his pale face, evil still lurking behind his brown eyes.

He had changed her life, and she still wasn't sure if it was for the better or worse.

The universe must have sensed her thoughts, as a two-day stretch brought a barrage of Jeremy Heston.

Yesterday she'd learned he had been shot in his room. Meanwhile, at her office, bigger news was about to break. An appointment had been arranged with someone named Cathleen Speidel, to discuss an "urgent matter." The name sounded familiar, but Linda couldn't quite remember why.

When the woman strolled through her office door, Linda immediately recognized her as the jury foreman from Jeremy's trial. The woman stared at Linda blankly from behind a pair of glasses. Her once-sandy hair had turned a deep shade of gray, the stress of the dramatic trial likely having worn her down.

"Hello, Mrs. Speidel, please have a seat." Linda stood to shake hands with the tall, stern woman.

"It's *Miss* Speidel," she said as she returned the handshake firmly.

"My apologies. What can I do for you today?" Before Linda had become a famous defense attorney, she spent time making small talk during appointments. Now, with a packed schedule, she had learned to cut to the chase.

"There's something I need to tell, and I wasn't sure who to tell. That district attorney always seemed to have a stick up his ass, but you're approachable. Maybe you can at least guide me in the right direction."

Linda noticed that Cathleen's hands were so chapped they looked like they might crumble into pieces if touched.

"I can certainly try. What's on your mind?"

Cathleen put a fist to her mouth, and looked to be running

through what to say. "I wanted to say something sooner, but was scared. Please understand."

Linda's senses heightened. She could tell from the woman's tone that something wasn't right.

"I was threatened during the trial," Cathleen said abruptly. "A man showed up at my house dressed in all black and told me if I didn't do everything in my power to make sure an insanity verdict was delivered that he'd kill my son. Then he told me my son's name and address."

Cathleen started to sob, tears flowing down her cheeks. Linda stared at her, unable to process the statement.

"Whoa, okay. Slow down." Linda handed her a tissue. "Someone threatened you to influence the outcome of the trial?"

"Yes," Cathleen managed through sniffles. "I wanted to say something at the time, but he choked me and said if I told anyone he would come back and it wouldn't be good for me."

"Jesus Christ," Linda whispered under her breath. She sat back. If this all checked out as true, Jeremy could possibly be freed through a vacated verdict. A judge would have to rule on the matter and could single-handedly decide his fate. The public would go nuts if Jeremy were to be freed after serving only a few months in the mental asylum. They would surely come after him if he wasn't granted witness protection. Linda pulled out a notepad.

"Okay, Ms. Speidel. I need you to tell me all the details from the beginning, including what happened in the deliberation room."

Linda pushed a tissue box across her desk. Cathleen crossed her legs, and stared at the wall behind Linda as she spoke.

"He came to me before the trial started. I was just at home,

103

unloading groceries from my car. It was nighttime, so I couldn't see too well."

Cathleen spoke flatly, clearly distraught by having to relive the experience.

"He came up behind me when I had my back turned to the main street in front of my house. He grabbed my throat, not enough to really choke me, but enough to where I couldn't talk. I can still feel his gloved fingers on my skin."

"What did he say to you?" Linda asked, flipping open her notepad.

"He said he knew I was on the Jeremy Heston jury and that I needed to make sure Jeremy received the insanity verdict. He said if I failed that he would fly to San Diego and slit my son's throat. Then he recited my son's address."

Cathleen's lips started to quiver, but she pushed through.

"He said I needed to become the jury foreman and sway everyone's opinions to vote not guilty. He also mentioned that he would leave me $100,000 as a thank you if I succeeded. And sure enough it was on my front porch the morning after the verdict was announced, in a brown box. All cash."

"$100,000?" Linda gasped. At first she had thought maybe an obsessed mental health advocate may have made the threats, perhaps a mentally ill person fighting the good fight for justice. But the mystery man had means, and that changed things. "What else did he tell you?"

"He said if I mentioned this to anyone that he'd come back to my house and it wouldn't be pretty for me. And that's it. He turned and sprinted away before I could even really process what happened."

Cathleen appeared to have calmed down, the tears having ceased, her body no longer trembling.

"I don't want you to mention this to anyone if possible. I just needed to tell someone before my head exploded from the guilt. I feel much better already."

"Ms. Speidel, I have to take this to the authorities. This is a major felony. They need to find the man who did this. I have a moral and professional obligation to bring this information forward, I hope you understand that."

She nodded slowly, still avoiding eye contact with Linda. "I understand. I thought that might be the case. Hell, I *knew* that would be the case. But I just couldn't take it anymore. I've booked a trip out of town next week. I need to get away."

"I understand. But you will need to be available for questioning. I have no doubt the detectives will want to interview you for themselves, so make sure you remain accessible."

"Understood," Cathleen said, and stood up.

"Was there anything else before you leave, Ms. Speidel?"

The woman shook her head. "No. Thank you for listening. You've helped me more than anything. Good luck finding the man who did this."

Cathleen turned and walked out of Linda's office.

Linda leaned back in her chair, still absorbing the info bomb that had just been dropped on her.

Something tells me whoever did this is the same person who sent me the documents to use against the prosecution's main psychologist. Someone was pulling strings all along.

She was glad now that she'd burned the documents the day after the trial ended. If those came to light, she could lose her license, and her fifteen minutes of fame would go down the shitter right along with her career. She had thrown the folder in her fireplace at home, sipping a glass of bourbon as she watched the evidence of her career's only dirty action turn into a pile of ash.

She picked up her phone and dialed Judge Zamora.

21

Chapter 21

Three weeks later, Dr. Carpenter sat in her office, typing up patient notes. She kept the office dim—she spent enough time under the bright lights of the patient rooms. Diagrams of the human brain decorated the walls in what was an otherwise plain office. Her desk faced two chairs, where she consulted with doctors and nurses on their findings regarding different patients.

The morning started to give way to the afternoon as she prepared to make her rounds and visit with patients. February had been a warm month, and this particular day had a springtime vibe, with the sun blaring, birds chirping, and no snow in sight.

Life had finally returned to normal following Jeremy Heston's shooting. It was all the talk around the hospital for the weeks following, from patients and staff alike, and she welcomed the normalcy with open arms. Jeremy had not shown any signs of regression, as she had thought he might. He was on track for returning as a regular member of society, although she would never let him see the light of day again.

Her office phone rang and she snapped it off the hook.

"This is Dr. Carpenter."

"Doctor, there are some men here to see you. They're with the FBI," the receptionist said.

"Okay, send them up."

FBI agents dropped in on occasion, to discuss high-profile or private cases they were working on. She had done a lot of work with the head of the Colorado chapter. But he was not with the group of three suited agents who entered her office, standing side by side.

"How can I help you gentlemen today?"

"Dr. Carpenter, we're going to need you to come with us," said the agent in the middle. She continued clicking around on her computer. "Now."

"I'm sorry, what is this regarding?" she asked. She had way too much shit to do today to be going anywhere with these men.

"Ma'am, this morning we arrested Dr. Adrian Siva. He's an associate of yours, right?"

Her heart sunk immediately. Adrian had guaranteed there wasn't any dirty business going on when he had called her to promise Heston as a patient.

She had no choice but to play along. "Yes. Is he okay?"

"He's been charged with jury tampering, among other matters regarding the Jeremy Heston trial."

He promised I wouldn't be tied to this in any way.

"Okay, I'm sorry to hear that, but what does it have to do with me?"

"Don't make this harder than it needs to be. We know he consulted with you on fixing the verdict to ensure Heston would be sent here under your care."

"*Consulted* with me? That is certainly not what happened. You have it all wrong. I don't know what you're talking about."

For all she knew they were making up these statements to try and get a confession from her.

The agent, a weasely man with a squeaky voice, pounced on Dr. Carpenter like a lion on its prey, slapping handcuffs around her wrist in a smooth motion.

"Harriet Carpenter, you're under arrest for colluding with jury tampering. You have the right to remain silent. Anything you say can and will be used against you in a court of law. You have the right to speak to an attorney, and to have an attorney present during any questioning. If you cannot afford one, one will be provided for you at government expense."

Siva, you fucking rat.

Her career would likely be over now, regardless of how this all ended. At the very least, she would be shunned by mental institutes around the country, and possibly have her license revoked.

"I want to speak with my lawyer," she demanded.

"You can do that down at our offices."

"I've done nothing wrong."

Holy shit, she thought as the reality of the situation sunk in. She would be taken into custody and not likely see the outside world for some time. She didn't know much about the law, but this surely had to be a felony.

The agent pulled her to her feet and guided her out of the office. Hospital staff gawked as they led her out of the hospital's main entrance.

"Business as usual!" she barked over her shoulder as the automatic doors closed behind her.

* * *

The agents borrowed a room at the Pueblo police station. Their main office was in Denver, but they needed to hear her statement before deciding whether to transport her to downtown.

She was fucked, and she knew the only way out of this situation without a long jail sentence would be to cooperate.

Two of the agents stayed with her in the interrogation room, the third likely behind the two-way mirror that overlooked the room.

"I received a phone call from Dr. Siva during the Jeremy Heston trial. I had never asked for anything from him—in fact, I hadn't spoken with him in a couple years. He asked if I'd be interested in having Jeremy Heston in my hospital. It wasn't something I had really thought about before he asked me, but I told him it would be intriguing to have Jeremy under my care. That's when he started talking about how he could make sure it happened. I asked him how. He told me to not worry about it."

"Then what?"

"That was that. He hung up and I didn't think anything of it. I certainly didn't know he would try and rig the verdict. He asked me if I was interested, I told him yes, and that was it."

The agents stared at her, their arms crossed as the interrogation light buzzed above their heads. Dr. Carpenter met their eyes and held her ground in the stare-down.

"I believe her," said the agent who had identified himself as Agent Livingston, the man who had arrested her. "Do you, Bell?"

Agent Bell nodded his head.

"We're going to hold you in custody. Even if your story is true, it's still collusion and you'll be tried in court."

"That doesn't seem fair. It's not like I asked him to rig it for Jeremy."

"Regardless, you asked for Heston, and you got him. You're technically an accomplice. You should have notified someone as soon as he started talking about how he could guarantee Heston delivered to your hospital." Agent Livingston spoke in monotone, showing no emotion.

"What about my lawyer?"

"You'll be able to contact your lawyer when we get to Denver."

The two agents left her alone in the room while they prepared for her transport to Denver.

It's all over. All because of Jeremy fucking Heston.

22

Chapter 22

Jeremy hadn't seen Dr. Carpenter in two days and had started to wonder what was going on. Whenever she had a day off, she always informed the patients ahead of time. The nurses had kept to their regular schedule, but didn't mention anything. He figured it was nothing to worry about.

He used his free time to continue planning his escape. Heightened security on campus made matters more difficult. If he made it outside, there would only be more obstacles waiting, ones he couldn't prepare for. He had also learned (thanks to being shot) that cameras covered every inch of the campus, meaning if he were to escape, he'd have to run like hell to get out of reach of a search party.

Time to implement cardio into my routine.

When he heard his door starting to unlock, he thought the nurse who had just left must had forgotten something.

Instead, his defense attorney walked in, opening a flood gate of memories. Her black briefcase reminded him of all the time they had spent together in court. She always had that briefcase, and whenever she clicked it open, he knew she meant business.

"Jeremy," she greeted him, walking toward his table with

confidence. "How have you been?" She set her briefcase on the table.

"Why, hello, Linda. This is a surprise."

"I wanted to visit sooner, but life and work have become so hectic since winning your case."

"Glad you've been having fun. I've been sitting in this room. It's better than jail, but still not where I belong."

"Well, that's why I'm here. I have some interesting news that I understand has not been shared with you yet."

"Oh?" Jeremy's eyebrows raised in high arches. "Interesting news?"

"Have you noticed Dr. Carpenter hasn't been around for a while?"

"Sure."

"Well, that's because she's in jail."

"Jail? For what?" Jeremy stood, anxious to know how this might affect his potential escape. If the doctor who had implemented all of the recent changes was in jail, would the hospital scale back to how things were before?

"Turns out she colluded with Dr. Adrian Siva to tamper with the jury and ensure your stay at this hospital."

She paused, and Jeremy felt an old, familiar tingle in his gut. *Destiny? Or rage?* It had been awhile since he felt either, but hearing Dr. Siva's name reignited a flame, after his visit with Jeremy.

"Dr. Siva? How is he tied into all of this?"

"He fixed the verdict, or at least tried to. We're not sure of his motive, or how successful he was. That's still being investigated. But the fact that he tampered with the jury and Dr. Carpenter's knowledge of the situation were enough to get them both arrested."

113

"What does that mean for the hospital?"

"There will be a new doctor coming in to take over. The state is currently interviewing doctors from around the world. Should be an announcement within the next week."

"Wait, does this mean I need to go through a different trial now?"

Linda shook her head.

"Not necessarily. Another trial is an option, but not one I think either side is willing to do. It was long, draining, and emotional. Since your verdict was technically not guilty, there's a slim chance you may be released. Remember, you're technically free to leave the mental hospital once a panel of psychiatrists unanimously agree that your mind has been rehabilitated."

Is this my way out? All because Dr. Siva went off the deep end.

Jeremy sat, silently processing the information.

"There's no way I'll be released that easily, right?"

"It's not likely, but it's a possibility. The fact that this is all coming out is crazy enough. There are a lot of moving pieces, so it's impossible to know what will happen."

"Can we file an appeal of any sort?"

"We can, but I would hold off and wait to see what happens. We don't want to file an appeal if it turns out the jurors were going to vote the same way regardless of the tampering. There's a lot of information that has yet to be revealed. This may all be a moot point, but I thought you should know what's going on. This is your life, after all."

"But the fact that there was tampering should count for something, right?"

"Yes, but at this point all we can file for is a retrial. Throw out the verdict and start over. I doubt a new jury would find you insane, that was honestly once in a lifetime. Even if the jury was tampered with, they found you not guilty, so there's no reason to pursue a new trial. We'll leave that to the D.A.'s office."

Jeremy had forgotten about Geoff Batchelor, the blond fuck who wanted him dead.

"How is the D.A. these days?" Jeremy asked mockingly.

"He's campaigning heavily for governor and I think he'll win. He's running on the Republican ticket and the Democrats can't seem to get their act together."

"Wow. Sorry to hear. I'm not a fan of his, for obvious reasons."

"Enough about him. How are you feeling about all this?"

"I'm still in shock. I think I know why Dr. Siva is behind all this. It might be a long shot, but I've had a long time to think this over."

Linda gestured for him to keep talking.

"In college, he always talked about changing the world, finding ways for psychology to help people. He seemed so desperate, especially with regard to mental health. He felt mentally ill people were treated wrongly in the justice system. And I agreed with him. Mentally ill people shouldn't be in jail or on death row, they need proper treatment. I think he saw my shooting as an opportunity to make an example. I'm not surprised to hear he tried to fix it to get me the insanity verdict. That, in his eyes, is fair treatment. He came to visit me here, a few weeks ago I think it was."

"He was in here?" Linda sat up stiffly. "He came into this room?"

"Yes. He sat right where you are and accused me of planning the entire shooting. Said that since there was no evidence of me planning it that I most certainly had to have planned it. He sounded a bit crazy if you ask me. Paranoid."

Jeremy realized he could spin this story to possibly favor him. Could he stretch it to where one might believe Dr. Siva had set up the entire thing himself? He planned to see.

Linda pulled out her phone and started typing. "I'm just taking some notes I think the FBI might want to know about. They gave me a pretty thorough briefing on the situation, since I was your defense attorney, and they didn't mention a known meeting with Dr. Siva coming here."

"I didn't think anything of it at the time, but since he left, I've had a nagging feeling inside that something wasn't right with him."

"When was this visit?"

Jeremy closed his eyes to run through his mental calendar. "Mid-January. Couldn't tell you an exact date, but it was a couple weeks after the new year."

Linda typed on her phone, looking like a zoned-out teenager in the middle of an intense texting conversation. Jeremy took her silence as an opportunity to ask about what had been bothering him for weeks.

"Have *you* heard from my parents by chance? Every time I ask to speak with them, I get told it'll be arranged and then it never happens."

"I haven't spoken with them since your trial ended. They sent me the final payment and that was that. The return address was from Arizona, which I found weird. Do you know if they moved?"

"I have no idea where they are. I haven't spoken to them since before the trial even started."

"I'll see what I can find out for you. They might just be

hanging low for a bit. Your parents received a lot of press during and after your trial. I'd imagine that was hard for them."

Jeremy thought about his mom, always shy and never wanting to speak with strangers. Having cameras and reporters in her face, questioning her about her mentally sick son, probably drove her into her own version of insanity.

"You've given me some valuable information. I need to get going, though—this is stuff that can't really wait, as this investigation is moving quickly. I'll be in touch as soon as I have an update. In the meantime, continue making progress. All of the notes say you're doing great since you've checked in."

"Thanks, Linda. Hope to hear from you soon."

She stood and left him alone. He wondered if she remembered his confession after the trial, when he admitted that this was all a big experiment to put mental illness to the ultimate test. She had vigorously denied it then, and likely erased any thought of it from her mind.

Jeremy stared out his window, absorbing the vast beauty of the world outside. Somewhere out there, an investigation into his trial was happening that could lead to his release. The world carried on with its daily drama as Jeremy grew older by the day, in the same room, looking at the same view, and reading the same book.

Just stay ready.

23

Chapter 23

For the first time in years, Jeremy felt hopeful for the future: there was an actual possibility of him being released from the mental institute.

Linda sent Jeremy a typed letter explaining the happenings of the investigation. The investigation had revealed that Dr. Siva did, in fact, sway a juror's vote, and threatened the juror to push their point of view on the others, with the goal of achieving a not guilty by reason of insanity verdict.

Geoff Batchelor was too overwhelmed with his gubernatorial campaign to retry the case. Linda speculated that he wouldn't want anyone in his office to potentially make worse mistakes than he had. Jeremy was in a mental facility, and leaving him there would have to suffice for the district attorney.

However, this left an open window for Linda to file an appeal and ask for a reduced stay in the mental institute. She could now make the argument that Jeremy was wrongfully sentenced as insane, and pin all of this on Dr. Siva.

The FBI had revealed that Dr. Siva had numerous files, both physical and electronic, in which he documented his desire to study a mentally insane murderer. His research had nothing to do with his private practice or the courses he taught at the university. It was a personal matter that he obsessed over.

Jeremy believed Dr. Siva had planted the seeds in his mind through a sort of hypnosis, to carry out a shooting in the name of science. Dr. Siva had the advanced knowledge to pull off such a feat.

Linda explained that Dr. Siva had kept extensive files on the trial, and made detailed notes about each juror. All of the notes, in fact, were about the jury. He didn't bother to write anything about the actual trial taking place.

He was scouting who he could shake. He had plenty of time to read the jurors and know who would be his best shot.

Once they had discovered this information, Dr. Siva decided to come clean and admit to everything he had done, likely hoping for an eventual reduced sentence for his cooperation. He admitted to leaving the envelopes of money for Jeremy's parents, the recommendation on which attorney to hire, and the stolen documents that he left for Linda. Dr. Siva was in jail on a $250,000 bond while a trial awaited him in the summer.

Linda was now under an investigation of her own, but with so much else going on, she didn't expect much to come out of it since she hadn't done anything technically illegal.

Dr. Carpenter had been released from custody with only a fine for her involvement. They believed her story that she had been unaware of what Dr. Siva was suggesting in his phone call with her, and received a figurative slap on the wrist with a $75,000 fine. She was promptly relieved of her duties by the institute.

Jeremy folded the letter and stuffed it back into its envelope. He'd received the letter already opened as the institute was required to check all incoming patient mail.

The new head doctor at the institute, Dr. Garza, was an old man, with a slightly hunched back, white hair bursting out of his ears, and skin so loose it appeared to be melting right off his bones.

His first meeting with Jeremy felt like speaking with the elder uncle at family gatherings, who reminisced about Vietnam and how great America used to be. Dr. Garza didn't even bring up Jeremy's file, or anything psychology-related, for that matter. He seemed to only be interested in getting to know Jeremy, assuring him that his past actions were over and done with. All they could do was move forward and help Jeremy with the mental recovery he needed.

"I've been in this line of work for fifty years now. I've worked with hundreds, maybe thousands, of soldiers suffering from post-traumatic stress disorder and depression," he told Jeremy. "And let me tell you, son, there's nothing worse for the human mind than war. It completely rewires your brain. Soldiers who return home unaffected are the true exceptions to the rule."

"I'm sorry to hear that, sir."

"What I'm trying to get at, Jeremy, is that your bipolar disorder is nothing compared to the patients I've helped in the past. I've helped rehabilitate tons of people who suffered from paranoia, delusions, and violent outbursts. I've received much criticism for letting patients back into society, but do you know how many times I've heard of a relapse?"

"Zero?"

Dr. Garza chuckled a hoarse laugh.

"Don't be naive. I've had three instances of a violent relapse. Out of more than three hundred cases. I know other doctors with a much worse record."

"Impressive." Jeremy wanted to ask him where he was going with all this, but decided to hold off and see.

"Do you think you're ready to return to society?" Dr. Garza asked, staring into Jeremy's soul with his brown, burning eyes.

Jeremy returned a tight-lipped grin. "I do. I never felt that coming here was necessary, but I understand why it needed to happen."

"I haven't done a formal assessment on you, but the reports I've read from Dr. Carpenter's notes show a steady and drastic improvement."

"Yeah, she had told me that too, but also said it was a long shot for me to get out."

"She was playing politics. No one wants to be the person who lets a murderer back on the streets. I don't blame her. There's a risk of having future blood on her hands, and that's something no doctor will chance."

Dr. Garza leaned back and placed a hand to his face, his elbow popping with every movement.

"I'm not most doctors. I don't believe in holding patients until they're old and can barely walk. What's the point of that? They may as well send you to jail if that's all they want. I believe rehabilitation can be reached in nearly every instance. I'm actually surprised the state hired me. They know my reputation, so I'm not sure why they'd want the PR nightmare that could come should I release you one day."

Jeremy licked his lips. *This guy is actually talking about releasing me. That's all I can ask for at this point.*

He would still plan his escape, but would also wait to see how the next few weeks played out with his new doctor. He might make life much easier.

"I'll begin my official assessment with you next week. From

there we'll see how much progress you've shown. If you can prove to me that you're no longer a threat to the public, then you can be released sometime in the next five years. If you can't show me that by then, it may be a lost cause."

Five years? Sorry, doc, I'm planning to be out of here this year. I have shit to do.

"Great, I appreciate your honesty, Dr. Garza. It's refreshing."

"I just want you to know my philosophy. Not giving a patient any sort of hope can hinder the healing process. Stay positive, keep moving forward with your progress, and we can get you back to normal."

Dr. Garza stood, his joints again screaming in protest, and wished Jeremy a good day before ambling out of the room.

24

Chapter 24

The two weeks that followed Dr. Garza taking over felt like a promotion for Jeremy. In the short span of time, he had been granted access to the common room whenever he pleased. The best perk, however, was the outdoors time he now enjoyed for two hours each day. With March approaching and the weather giving a tease of warmth, Jeremy spent his outdoors time pacing around the courtyard.

The courtyard was enclosed by the hospital buildings that formed a U shape around the grass, tables, and benches. He had hoped that once he saw the outside of the building he'd be able to devise a better escape plan, but it only crushed his spirits when he found there was literally no way out.

He did discover that having access to the courtyard could make a diversion easier. Causing a scene outside could leave the inside more accessible. Dr. Garza had downgraded the security coverage, citing Dr. Carpenter's "knee-jerk" reaction to an outlier of a situation.

Outdoors time was supervised by three guards who stood along the entrance to the commons area. They rarely left their posts, but would have no choice should some patients break into a fight.

The frustrating part for Jeremy was trying to get his friends' support. All they wanted to do was work on those stupid puzzles. He suggested they take the puzzle outside and get fresh air while working their minds. They all stared at him and called him obscenities before returning to the puzzle. He considered telling them he was planning an escape, and that they could treat the task as a puzzle of its own. Perhaps then he could get their help.

He really wished he could write down his thoughts. There were too many scenarios he had played out in his mind to mentally keep track of. Maybe the new doctor wouldn't read his new notebook; he seemed to trust him enough.

* * *

The next day Jeremy pulled Damon aside, asking him for five minutes of his time away from the goddamn puzzles. Jeremy thought Damon had his shit together more than the others. He had also spent more time in the hospital and would know the facility best.

The two walked outside, the sun reflecting brightly off their all-white scrubs. Jeremy led them to the furthest point from the guards before speaking.

"Damon, I need to tell you something, and you might be able to help."

"Okay." Damon nodded, eyes bulging.

"I'm planning an escape," Jeremy said in a lowered voice.

"How brave of you," Damon said, unimpressed. "What's

your plan?"

"I was wondering if you guys might be able to stage a fight out here in the courtyard, then I'll slip out the emergency exit."

"You know the emergency exit only unlocks when the fire alarm is pulled, right? They'll be on to you."

"I'm fast. I've seen our guards. I'm pretty sure they won't be able to catch me."

Damon smiled like a madman as he nodded his head.

"That's a nice plan, but it won't work."

"How do you know?"

"I've tried it. I started a fight, had people hitting each other all over this very spot. I slipped back inside and the guard on duty saw me and kept a close eye on me. As soon as I started taking a step toward the long hallway, he started to follow me. The security here may not seem that tight, but they are definitely trained to be a step ahead."

"So what, there's no way?"

"You ask that like there should be. This is a mental hospital, one of the biggest in the country, and now, thanks to you, the most famous one. You really think there's a simple way to just walk out the doors, hop a fence, and hitchhike down I-25 without anyone caring? They told us you're a really smart guy, but it doesn't sound like you've thought this through."

"There's always a way," Jeremy insisted. "Sure, the guards may be a step ahead, but they are still humans. They can make mistakes—they *will* make mistakes. It's just a matter of finding a way to exploit those mistakes and slip through the cracks."

Damon kept his devilish grin. "Why do you want to escape so bad? What's out there in the world for you? A girl?"

Jeremy thought of Jamie and how he'd love to have just five minutes to explain everything. Since she had walked out of his life he'd never gotten the closure he wanted. And then, just a few months after she broke off the relationship, she would have had to endure seeing his face all over the news and social media.

"No, there's no girl." Jeremy gave Damon a friendly slap on the arm. Their conversation felt more like two friends talking about their weekends instead of two mental patients discussing an escape plot.

"Well, then, why leave here? You get fed, play with friends, get to go outside, all rent-free. You could say life in here is better than a normal life, with all its responsibilities."

"I think you've been here too long with that crazy talk."

"I know this is a boring and repetitive life. Nothing is ever new and exciting. Before here I was a blackjack dealer in Vegas. Now that was a fun life, my friend."

"Don't you want to go back to that life? Have fun again?"

"Nah. It was fun, but I'm too old now to keep up with the Vegas life. The hours were horrid, and the lights and bells would only give me a headache. Shit, I really do sound like an old man."

Jeremy turned his body to face Damon straight on and took a deep breath. He never thought he'd share this information with anyone, but the most desperate of times meant that anything was fair game. *Just go for it.*

"I need to tell you something," he said, and thought back to the time he had made the same confession to Linda, who all but laughed in his face. "You may or may not believe me, but I don't have a mental problem."

"Of course not." Damon chuckled. "None of us in here do." *Relax. Explain yourself.*

"No, really. This sounds crazy, but my shooting was carefully planned to make sure I ended up in here. I'm a psychologist, and I wanted to run an experiment to show the world that mental illness needs to be taken seriously. It always gets blown over and dismissed, and it seemed so unjust."

Damon stared at him blankly, but Jeremy caught a twinkle in his eyes that suggested he might be considering what he had just said.

"Sounds like bull if you ask me," Damon finally responded. "What person in their right mind would risk their entire life for something like this? The odds of you ending up in here had to be less than one percent."

"I'm the kind of person to take that risk."

"Yeah, a bipolar psychopath. You probably planned this attack when you were in one of your bad moods and woke up the next day in jail, right?"

Jeremy thought back to that weekend, and Damon was right. He couldn't remember much after the bodies had fallen and the police arrived. He'd figured the trauma of carrying out such an action would have that effect, so he never thought twice about it. In fact, thinking back to the couple months leading up to the shooting, Jeremy couldn't remember much. His visits to his Uncle Ricky's property in the mountains seemed in retrospect like he was on autopilot.

The thought concerned him. He couldn't recall a time in life when he'd struggled with memory. He could remember specific events during his childhood, like his first basketball game, for example. He could still smell the hot dogs and nachos that filled the concourse, the *ooohs!* and *aaahs!* of the crowd whenever the Nuggets made or missed a shot.

Much of his life's memories remained graphically detailed in his mind, but why not any of his massacre planning? He remembered *being* at his uncle's cabin, but couldn't even give any details about what he had done there.

You're not bipolar. Your mind was just occupied with the task at hand. Happens to the best of us. You remember cramming for exams in college? Same thing.

Except it wasn't. He could recall those exams, could taste the rum he would sip during his all-night study sessions, could hear the sound of Jamie's voice on the phone telling him to get some sleep or he'd pass out during the exam. Even those memories slapped him across the face as a new reality started to settle in.

There's a large chunk of time I can't account for. But there has to be an explanation.

Jeremy would never admit to Damon that maybe he was right. "I'm not bipolar. I know perfectly well what I'm doing and what I was doing at the time."

"Tell me more about this plan of yours. If it sounds plausible, then maybe I'll help you out." Damon stared at Jeremy with serious eyes.

"Okay."

Damon nodded, and gestured for Jeremy to proceed.

"My initial plan was to get the insanity verdict, and by some miracle it actually happened."

"A miracle? I thought you meant for it to happen."

"I did. I also quickly learned in jail and during the trial that it wouldn't be so straightforward. Listening to the testimony against me made me question my own sanity. But I had a good lawyer and an even better psychologist to testify on my behalf. It ended up working out. My goal was to start a trend, where mental illness would be discussed more in the justice system and recognized as an epidemic. It may have happened for all I know, but I can't know for sure until I get out of here."

"And what will you do when you get out of here?"

"I'll research what's been happening since my verdict. I want to write a book about how I was treated in jail, the legal process, and then, of course, my time here."

Damon brushed his chin with thin, scraggly fingers. "And when this is all said and done, what will you have achieved? People will still see you as a mass murderer."

"My achievement will be shedding light on the ugliness that lies beneath our society. Did you know before my shooting, there was an average of one mass shooting every day in this country? A mass shooting is defined as a single incident where four or more people are shot. One *every* day. It's become so normalized, that only the big shootings are reported anymore. That's why I did mine in my office. It was something everyone would be able to relate to. Anyone can take a gun to work and wipe out an entire company if they want to."

"I know you're a psychologist, but why take on mental health? Don't you see that guns are the problem? Mass shootings require a gun."

"Well, no shit, guns are a problem. But there's no fixing that issue. I decided when that kid killed a classroom of first graders and nothing changed, that it'll never be resolved. Our society is too arrogant to look at other countries that have virtually no gun deaths. That arrogance is going to get all of us killed—and that's why I decided to focus on mental health. If I can get people to start discussing it as a legitimate issue, that's a step in the right direction."

Damon crossed his arms and looked to the ground, then spoke quietly. "I have a plan I believe will work. It's yours to use, and I'm ready to try it."

Jeremy felt a sudden rush of adrenaline. *He's in. He wants to help.*

"What do we do?" Jeremy kicked the dirt, hoping to give the impression to the guards watching that they were just a couple of guys having a normal conversation.

"I can't tell you. If I tell you, you'll back out. Just be ready to run tomorrow."

"Run?" *Holy shit. Tomorrow?* The sudden escalation of his escape caught him by surprise. He would have never expected to be discussing this as a reality so soon.

"How else do you expect to get out of here? You'll know when the time comes, you'll have maybe a ten-second window to recognize it and sprint for that emergency exit at the end of the hall. Make sure to pull the alarm on your way out."

"Tell me what the plan is. I can help." Jeremy took a stern tone with Damon. He was a good friend and Jeremy didn't want to see him jeopardize himself.

"I'm not telling. After lunch, be ready, keep an eye on me. When you get out, you need to make it count. I expect to see big things from you."

"I won't forget you. And please find me when you make it out."

"Not likely to make it out any time soon, but I'll keep that in mind. Now as far as your escape. When you exit the emergency door, you'll be facing the west side of campus. You'll have one building to run around and there's a small fence you should be able to jump easily. Jump that fence and sprint south. It's a mile and a half to an abandoned rail yard. There's hundreds of train cars. Hide out there until the time feels right, then go two more miles west to Prairie Avenue. There's a huge thrift store on that street that you should be able to enter without getting attention. Change into a normal outfit and figure it out from there."

Jeremy filed mental notes on everything Damon had just told him. "How do you know all this?"

"Well, when you've made it to the top as a patient at this fine institution, you can get Internet privileges two whole times each year."

Jeremy noted the obvious sarcasm. "And you studied the map around the hospital?"

"Every time. We get a strict thirty minutes to surf the Web. I always study the map of Pueblo. Like I said, I've been looking at escape options for a long time. At my age, there's no way I'd make it far. But, you're in shape to run over a mile for your life. And I believe in your vision. Sometimes you can just sense what's in a man's heart."

"Thank you. I never thought I'd tell anyone my story, let alone have someone believe and support it."

"Those of us on the inside are the only ones who understand how mental illness really is. We never get the chance to share that with the world, which is why you have to. Remember my directions, and be ready after lunch tomorrow."

A fluttering filled Jeremy's chest as they ended their conversation and returned inside to the puzzle.

Tomorrow after lunch. Destiny.

25

Chapter 25

Damon devoured his lunch. Chicken and mashed potatoes had never tasted better. He understood why prisoners on death row were offered a request for their final meal. Knowingly eating a final meal made every flavor burst with deliciousness. When death awaited, it was much easier to take joy in the little things.

Thirty pills were stuffed in his pants pocket after his final extraction from his pillow the night before, and he reached in for one when he finished his final bite of potato, savoring the shred of garlic seasoning that clung to his tongue.

Pills take about 45 minutes to process, he recalled. Taking the pills now, at 12:30, would allow the show to start at a quarter past one. Bubbles felt like they were boiling in his stomach as his nerves cranked into high gear. It wasn't the action, but rather the not knowing what would happen, that made him sick.

He saw Jeremy peering at him from across the room. His ambitious friend had been taking his planning seriously; his body appearing chiseled compared to the blubber of everyone else in the room. Jeremy looked like he might be able to steamroll a security guard if it came down to it. Desperation can make a person do truly incredible things.

Damon raised his cup of water to Jeremy. *Cheers to you. This better work out, or help me God I'll come back here and haunt your room until you really do go insane.*

A quick glance around the room showed no one paying attention to him after Jeremy returned to his conversation with Edgar and Dusty. The guard overlooking the room stared lifelessly at the TV on the wall showing reruns of *The People's Court.*

He popped the first pill into his mouth and swallowed it with a gulp of water. He pulled the next pill out of his pocket and repeated the process, doing so thirty times until he reached into his pocket and felt nothing but cloth. His eyes jumped around the room, paranoid, but no one had noticed him.

Have mercy on me, God, he thought, having never prayed before in his life. The pills sat in his stomach, awaiting their chance to attack his central nervous system.

* * *

When the clock struck one, the nurses made their rounds to pick up the food trays and restore the commons area back from eating to socializing. Damon remained in his chair and stared at the wall. The room spun around him, even when he closed his eyes. He also felt incredibly sleepy. More sleepy than he'd ever been. If a bed had been nearby he would've happily dived into its cotton caress and had the best sleep of his life.

There was no bed, though. Only a spinning room and hiccups that started to make their way up to his swelling throat. If he gave into them, it would only lead to vomiting the pills and throwing a major wrench into the escape plan.

Keep them down. Just a few more minutes and it'll all be over.

He grabbed his cup of water with a hand trembling like a Parkinson's patient. Droplets spilled on the table as he fumbled to get it to his mouth for one final sip. The coolness of the water felt like a monsoon pouring over a desert, as his tongue had gone dry and numb from the medication. His eyes felt like heavy, bulging boulders trying to fall out of his face as the room started to spin faster.

Breathing felt like someone had pinched his nostrils shut, allowing single particles of oxygen to seep their way into his desperate lungs. His lungs tingled as he tried harder to inhale, and they felt like they'd been lit on fire inside his chest.

Damon stood, surprising himself that he was able to get to his feet. Jeremy had remained at the puzzle table, watching him like a vulture ready to pounce on its prey. *He's gonna do it,* Damon thought as he choked down an aggressive belch.

He tried to take a step toward the middle of the room, but his entire body turned numb and he couldn't do so much as wiggle his fingers. He stood like a statue while no one besides Jeremy noticed him. Beneath the numbness, his heart slammed against his rib cage, and the weight of the world pressed down on his lungs. A buzzing sound, like a fly you can't quite locate in your house, filled his head as a bead of sweat trickled off his forehead and down his face. Now he thought his eyes were actually bulging from their sockets, as a nurse finally realized something wasn't right.

"Damon?" Her soft voice echoed through the depths of his fading mind. He remained frozen until something that felt like a monstrous punch knocked him hard in the chest, and sent him sprawling to the ground in a lifeless thud.

Three nurses rushed to him, screaming for help. The guards who covered the perimeter of the room dashed toward the huddle of nurses, and the last thing Damon saw was a clear path to the end of the hallway, where Jeremy Heston would make his run for freedom.

26

Chapter 26

Damon fingered the inside of his pillow through a small slit. The moment had finally arrived. After feeling a constant nausea during his first three years in the institute, he'd decided to take matters into his own hands.

It's been a good run, he thought. Jeremy was right. He had become "institutionalized." He wouldn't last two seconds outside of the hospital. The very thought of it sent chills up his back.

Damon had always known that some day a new patient would come along, seeking a way out of the hospital. He put tons of mental preparation, observation, and planning into a fool-proof method. The only problem was it would never be for *his* escape. The task required would never be considered by another patient. Sure, there were solid friendships around the hospital, but nothing serious enough to lay down a life for one another.

He had started hiding his pills inside his pillowcase after those grueling first three years. He stuffed them as far into the center as possible, jamming them through the rough cotton. Once the medication had been completely flushed from his system, the nausea also disappeared.

The doctors told him the pills never caused nausea as a side effect, but he knew better. Without the medication, he could eat meals without feeling sick, and his mind felt sharper and better equipped to concentrate.

Damon had been diagnosed with paranoid schizophrenia, and assumed he would spend an eternity (if not the rest of his life) in the luxurious confines of Rocky Mountain Mental Health Institute. It was no way to live, and he knew that one day enough would be enough, so he saved the pills.

Overdosing was painless, according to the scientific reports he'd read online. The body simply turned off and faded into a deep sleep from which it would never wake. Should he ever decide to call it quits, he'd access his plethora of pills, and pop them into his mouth like Skittles. Then he'd be free. Free for whatever comes in the afterlife. He hoped it was a second chance to try it all again, to learn from the mistakes that landed him in a building with the delusional members of society.

His discussion with Jeremy left him inspired and ready to support the hospital's most famous patient in history. Years of closely studying the hospital's protocols for nearly every situation imaginable had led to his confidence in his plan. He could attract everyone's attention in one drastic action, all by himself. It only required two people: himself and the escaping patient.

Damon's desire to escape had waned over the recent years. He came to accept that he wouldn't be leaving the hospital unless he could successfully execute an escape. At his age now, was it worth it to stage such a dramatic escape, only to live the rest of his life being hunted by the authorities?

"Fuck that," he told himself. At the hospital he had it all:

meals, entertainment, and friends. His family had disowned him anyway, so he'd have no one to turn to on the outside.

Still, he kept his plan in his back pocket for the right time. And the right person. Surely no one would want to perform his role in the escape; it had to be him. Some might call it the ultimate sacrifice; he considered it a way to fast forward to his inevitable ending.

That's a wrap, folks. Thank you and drive home safely.

Jeremy had everything that met Damon's criteria. He'd had a hunch when he heard the mass murderer was coming to the hospital. Meeting him in person only strengthened that suspicion. Jeremy had ambition, hunger, and just enough lunacy to be able to escape. However, his vision and plan for what he would do after escaping was what ultimately convinced Damon. Jeremy showed a genuine desire to change the world. Mental hospital patients had a bad reputation in society, but there was no reason for it. Their illness was just as legitimate as those who enter a medical hospital. All they want is to get better. Even if they had done bad things, patients simply wanted a way to overcome the hell that lived trapped within their skulls.

When Jeremy spoke, Damon could feel the truth tied to each word. His bipolar friend wasn't feeding him a line of bullshit. Jeremy Heston meant what he said, and, damn it, he would do what he said if he could just get out of this cursed building.

Damon studied the ten pills he had pulled out and wondered what would come next. It couldn't be worse than the hospital, but it might not necessarily be better. The unknowing would have frightened him at one point in life, but he was far past that. The little white circles in his hand seemed to be staring at him, trying to speak. Perhaps they would once they were in his system.

He laid the pills out on his table and returned to the pillow to pull out ten more, lining all twenty next to each other before piling them under a stack of papers he kept on the table. He patted them like a person meeting a small dog for the first time.

"Tomorrow, my friends. Tomorrow is the day."

27

Chapter 27

Even though Jeremy could access the commons area after breakfast, he decided to wait. The oatmeal churned in his stomach and he worried he might spew it all over his room. His paranoia reached the point where he couldn't even look the nurse in the eyes. He feared they might have been on to him, that one of the guards had overheard the conversation in the courtyard and would beat Jeremy to the punch, to embarrass him and send an example to the rest of the patients.

This is a one and done chance. It either succeeds and the next chapter comes, or it fails and I'll never see the light of day again.

The nerves he felt reminded him of the morning of March 11, 2016, except this time around so many factors were out of his control. Sure, Damon had given him the route to follow, but Jeremy had never seen the outside of the hospital, with the exception of the parking lot and the view from his fourth-floor window. He also had no idea what the fuck Damon was going to do. "Be ready after lunch" couldn't be any more vague for a plan that required a massive amount of research and planning. He had no choice but to trust Damon, and that contributed to his uneasiness.

If he went down to the commons area now, Damon would be there with the others, working on their damned puzzles. Jeremy would have every urge to pull Damon aside and demand the plan. The last thing he needed was to piss off the only person in the world willing to help him. Sometimes trust is all you can rely on.

So instead, Jeremy paced circles in his room and recited the directions for his escape route, drilling them into his mind like a student cramming for a test. One wrong turn could mean the difference between a free life and capture, so the route had to be perfect in his mind. He planned to step foot outside, in a world he hadn't yet seen.

What kind of fucked-up mission is this? he wondered. Jeremy had come to terms while in jail that he had failed in the execution of his plan. All of his focus had been on the shooting and the couple days after being arrested, and he had never considered preparation for the trial or mental hospital. It was amateur and lackluster planning, he realized, thinking back. But now he was exactly where he planned to be, by accident, and it would all came down to the words and actions of a paranoid schizophrenic.

Jeremy wanted nothing more than to curl up in bed and forget all about it. The doubts of his mission were at the surface of his mind. Looking back at the last two years, he realized what a naive and silly plan he had created. People hated him. No sympathy was created when he received the insanity verdict. No one jumped up to offer help to heal his mind. Presumably, most wanted him dead, while nearly everyone wanted him in jail instead of the loony bin.

And it was exactly that arrogance toward mental illness that had fueled Jeremy's fire to prove everyone wrong. So what if they all hated him? There were plenty of people in history that changed the world despite being hated.

When the nurse came back at ten, Jeremy let her know that he wanted to go down to the commons area. His jitters wouldn't be leaving any time soon, so he might as well see what kind of information he could get from Damon. The nurse led him to the area and, as suspected, Damon sat in a circle with his crew as they mulled over different puzzle pieces.

"Hey guys," Jeremy said as he approached.

"Hey, Jeremy," Edgar and Dusty said in unison, without looking up. Damon kept his focus on the puzzle and remained silent.

"Damon, can I have a word please?" Jeremy asked in a soft voice, not wanting to come across as pushy.

"Yes, one sec," Damon responded dismissively. He lifted a piece from the pile in front of him, examined it, and snapped it into its proper place in the puzzle, which looked to be a scenic view of a beach.

Damon stood and walked to the courtyard without a glance at Jeremy, who promptly followed him outside.

"Hey, man. Just wanted to see if we're still on? I've been memorizing the directions you gave me."

Damon nodded and rubbed his temples. "Yes, we're on."

Jeremy sensed uncertainty from his escape partner.

"Everything okay?" he asked, putting a hand on Damon's shoulder.

"Yeah...I just never thought this day would come. It's been only in my imagination for all these years. I don't want to call it a dream of mine, because it's really not some crazy fantasy."

"Why won't you tell me what you're doing? Won't it only help if I know what I'm looking for?"

"I'm sure it would. But if I tell you, you'll call it off. You're a good guy. I can sense it. I also believe your story. You're different from any patient I've met. There's something special to this whole thing that's bigger than both of us. I, for one, want to thank you for what you're doing. I don't think we'll see it in our lifetimes, but there will be a day when mental health patients are treated no differently than people going to the emergency room with a broken bone. It's a real illness that can be treated like anything else. *We* see that. We *know* that."

"Thank you, Damon. I appreciate that. It's refreshing to know there are others who feel the same way."

"I mean it, Jeremy. If you succeed in carrying out your plan, whether that's writing a book or whatever you decide, I believe history will remember you as a pioneer for mental health. There will be mental hospitals named after you."

"I think that's a bit much. I did kill thirteen people, and that'll never be forgiven."

"It might not be forgiven, but it'll be forgotten. There will only be more mass shootings, some with a higher death toll, I'm sure. One day your shooting will look insignificant compared to the ones that haven't happened yet. Were you living in the state during the Columbine shooting?"

"I was a kid, but yes."

"If you go outside of Colorado, you'll find people who don't know about Columbine, or may have forgotten about it. It's a footnote in history now. The world moves on. You may always be hated here locally, but if you can get out of the state and try to spread your word elsewhere, you can succeed. Find a liberal city where people are willing to listen, and see what happens."

Jeremy hadn't considered this before. Perhaps he should've been consulting Damon since they first met. He had the wisdom and seemed to have thought this whole thing through better than Jeremy had over the last six months. With only a couple more hours of having Damon as a resource, he decided now was the time to pick his brain for all it was worth.

"My big concern is how to go about this. I'm going to be on the run. Even if I'm in another state and someone sees me in public, I can be detained and sent back here."

"True. You'll need to lay low. If that means living on the streets until the news of your escape blows over, then so be it. There are plenty of small towns where you can find landlords willing to rent a room to you without any sort of background check. I'd say go find a small town, get a job doing dishes or some sort of cleaning, build up not only money but also a new identity. When you leave here, you should right away begin thinking of who you want to be. You can't be Jeremy Heston anymore. Jeremy Heston will be known as a mass murderer and asylum escape artist. Change your name, get a new look, maybe even change the way you speak. Do *not* visit any friends or family from your past life. You have no friends or family now."

Jeremy scrunched his brow at the thought. "I owe it to my parents to explain. I never got the chance in jail."

"Nope," Damon said bluntly. "You can't. No one can come in contact with you. It could cause a scene, they may report you, you have no idea how they will react if they see you."

Jeremy hated to hear that, but recognized its truth.

"I appreciate that. There's a lot I haven't considered yet." Jeremy felt unsure about his escape, but figured he would always feel that way, no matter how ready he truly was. "Another concern is having an audience. Sure, I can write a book, or start a blog, but how am I supposed to know if there are even people who care?"

"People care. More than you'd imagine. Do you know how many people in this very hospital haven't had visitors in years? Almost everyone. It's not that the family doesn't care; they don't understand. The thought of having a mentally ill relative makes them uneasy, and they end up shunning them. It really is a matter of showing people that it's nothing to fear. People fear what they don't understand and this is no different."

Jeremy soaked in all the information. It seemed as if Damon had been placed in his life to make sure he saw his grand plan through.

"On that note, are you ready to get out of here?" Damon asked confidently.

"Yes. I just wish you'd tell me what to expect."

"Keep your eye on me after lunch and be ready. When you realize it's time, don't hesitate, don't try to help me, don't be a hero. Just turn and run like hell."

* * *

Patients were allowed to enjoy lunch in the commons area, to socialize while they ate. Sharing a meal with friends was one of the many things Jeremy ended up realizing he had taken for granted. He reminisced about the many nights he'd spent with his old friend, Ronnie, during his college days, eating and drinking until the sun came up. They had their differences, but he wished he could go back to those days when life seemed so simple, and dreams felt achievable.

Instead, he sat in the commons of a mental institution

picking at his potatoes and chicken. He joined Edgar and Dusty at the same table where they did their puzzle, only it now had a tablecloth draped over the top so they could eat their meals without destroying their life's work.

Damon had told them he needed some time to himself and opted to sit across the room where no one would bother him. No one minded, but when he winked at Jeremy, his heart sunk because he knew whatever Damon had planned would be underway soon.

Jeremy forced his food down, not knowing when his next meal would come. His arms and legs trembled with each passing bite, knowing every second was one closer to the biggest obstacle of the last two years of his twisted experiment. He didn't even feel this nervous in the moments before slaughtering his coworkers and friends.

What's he gonna do? he wondered as he watched his new confidant across the room. Damon appeared to have no issue with his appetite, as he rapidly scooped spoonfuls of food into his mouth, sitting in the corner like a loner and paying no attention to those around him.

Jeremy saw the clock on the wall read 12:30 and knew his destiny waited just around the corner.

28

Chapter 28

What the fuck?

Jeremy watched Damon fall to the ground. His eyes had rolled back into his head before his knees gave out. *Is this really the plan?*

Jeremy waited cautiously, watching the panicked nurses shouting and running to the limp pile of flesh on the ground.

All attention was on Damon, from the nurses to the three guards, and all the other patients had formed a huddle around the scene.

This is it.

Jeremy looked behind him, toward the hallway that led to the emergency exit, where not a soul stood in sight. How could Damon have known this would work? Had he tested something similar to see how the staff and patients would react? Regardless, Jeremy stood on legs of Jell-O, frozen in place.

GO, GOD DAMN IT, THIS IS IT!

His instincts kicked in and he started toward the hallway, keeping his stare on the crowd. All the guards and nurses crowded around the group of patients as one nurse performed

CPR to try and revive Damon. His body didn't flinch once.

Jeremy turned back to the hallway, saw the glass door at the end, the day's sunlight welcoming him, and bolted for it like a baseball player trying to steal a base. The walls and doors passed in a colorful blur as the light illuminating the door grew brighter with each stride. He hadn't run at full speed for quite some time and it felt great. His feet seemed to glide above the ground as he ran gracefully toward the exit.

When he reached the door, he found the fire alarm on the wall, and pulled at its white lever in a quick motion, pausing for the slightest moment until he heard its siren scream throughout the building. The door made a *clunk!* sound as it unlocked, the most beautiful sound Jeremy had ever heard. Adrenaline flooded his veins as he reached for the push bar to open the door, stumbling out of the hospital, where the blinding sunlight made him shield his eyes.

The fresh air filled his lungs. He'd spent time in the court-yard, but the sense of freedom made the air feel different, more pure. The piercing, high-pitched screech drowned out as the door closed gently behind him.

The building Damon had mentioned stood in front of him, towering in its concrete facade. There were only a couple people walking around the campus, none of whom appeared to be security, so Jeremy sprinted toward the building. Time felt at a standstill as he ran, the whooshing sounds of the breeze filling his head as his sneakers thumped on the concrete below.

He reached the back of the building and saw the fence Damon had referenced. Without slowing, Jeremy lunged for it, planting a foot in one of the holes of the chain-link fence and thrusting his body over the top. His feet hit the dirt with a heavy force that sent vibrations up to his knees. He lost balance and tumbled like a boulder down the side of a mountain for ten feet before he popped back up and broke into another sprint.

A quick glance over his shoulder saw a couple of security guards running from the hospital and shouting at Jeremy. He figured he had a football field's length between him and the guards, not factoring the fence into the equation.

Jeremy ran for the neighborhood that waited half a mile ahead. It was all dirt between him and the first houses. He ran, his ankles twisting on the many bumps and dips of the open field. Some sent waves of pain throughout his legs. As long as no ligaments tore, he'd be fine.

It took him four minutes to run that half-mile to the first house, which had a backyard with a kid's swing set, a miniature swimming pool, and a covered patio he would have loved to sit down in and drink an ice-cold lemonade.

The cool air stung his lungs with each inhale as his body fought him to slow down. A throbbing cramp formed in his gut as he heaved for every bit of oxygen his body would allow.

You have to slow down, he thought, but knew damn well that he had to push through to the finish line. According to Damon, it would be another half-mile through the neighborhood until he reached the rail yard. *How long until the hospital calls the police? Then how long until they actually arrived to the neighborhood with a full search party?*

He had no way of knowing, but the quiet neighborhood soothed his racing thoughts. Instead of sprinting, Jeremy ran at a normal pace, as one might for an evening run around the park.

The neighborhood was deserted. It was a weekday, with everyone at work or school. Aside from his white scrubs, he looked no different than a resident of the neighborhood out for an afternoon run. The news would take time to spread, so even if someone did see him, they wouldn't necessarily make the connection in the moment.

You're almost free. Just. Keep. Fucking. Going.

Jeremy kept moving. The adrenaline had yet to wear off. Even though his body protested, his mind had its eye on the prize and persisted forward. After a minute of running at a regular speed, he returned to sprinting, his legs numb as they covered another half-mile at a pace he hadn't run since high school.

Have they called the police yet? he wondered. It had to have been ten minutes between his escape and his reaching the furthest edge of the neighborhood. Surely they saw the direction he had run and would have sent a unit to scope out the neighborhood. It all remained eerily silent as he approached the final house before a new dirt field led down to the abandoned rail yard.

Won't they look for me here? It seems obvious.

Damon hadn't let him down so far with his instructions, and Jeremy would just have to trust him, that everything would work out.

Hope you're making it through, buddy.

He gawked at the hundreds of train cars spread across the rail yard, some passenger, but mostly cargo. He'd have to climb into one of them and hide out for the next day or two until the buzz died down. People around town would be on the lookout, so he'd have to make his moves at night. How cold would it be at night anyway? The current day felt like the low 60s, meaning nighttime would be somewhere in the 30s or 40s. His scrubs wouldn't suffice to keep him warm; he'd have to find a store with a changing room where he could swap outfits and leave. Shoplifting on his first day back in society wasn't a wise plan, but he had no other choice. His uniform would make him stand out in any public setting.

When Jeremy decided the coast was clear, he crossed the street and broke into a final run toward the grouping of train cars. They waited 200 yards away, downhill, making the final leg of his journey much easier than the rest had been. His thighs and hamstrings welcomed the downhill path.

He arrived to the outermost row of train cars and walked between them, browsing the massive steel boxes like he was strolling through the mall. The rows of various-colored train cars looked to go on forever, so Jeremy walked five rows in before looking for the car he would call home for the next couple of days.

A faded yellow one with UNION PACIFIC written in giant red font on its side grabbed his attention. He found its attached ladder, climbed it, and from the top could see the neighborhood behind him, still abandoned, and still no sign of the police. Inside the train car, the walls were powdered black, likely a former coal carrying car. Jeremy thought rolling around in it and turning his white outfit a darker shade would only help his cause. Laying in coal dust might also throw off his scent should the police bring bloodhounds. He wasn't sure if they would go to that extreme, but he couldn't rule it out. The laws and procedures regarding a mental asylum escapee were another item to add to the long list of things he wished he had researched.

Jeremy had always imagined the inside of a cargo car to be a straight drop to its bottom, but was delighted to find that each end of it had a ramp that sloped to the center. He pulled himself over the edge and dropped a yard to land on top of the ramp. His shoes failed to grip the floor and he slid in slow motion to the bottom, clawing with his fingers to get a grip, and leaving a long, winding trail of yellow in the soot, above the two streaks where his feet had dragged. Having been in the train for less than a minute, his clothes and skin already showed coal dust clinging to him.

From the bottom he looked up. The piercing blue sky looked down at him as he stood in silence. An airplane passed far above, and he wondered about the passengers who might be looking out of their window to the earth below, oblivious that a mass murderer was posting up camp in the abandoned rail yard.

29

Chapter 29

Before word spread about Jeremy's escape, Connor had once again been called into the Pueblo Police Station, and this time he could sense that the interrogating detectives were trying to get a confession from him. They had even suggested he take the day off from work, which he begrudgingly obliged.

"Did you know the mental hospital is less than half a mile from your apartment building?" the detective asked under a blinding light that hung above their heads.

"No, sir. I know it's close. I can see it from my window."

"Piecing together a crime is a difficult task, Mr. Chappell. So far, all signs point back to you. Your location near the crime, your timing for a job in Pueblo, it all seems a bit planned. We originally chalked it up as a coincidence, but that's looking less likely."

Connor lost control of his thumping heart as it tried to break through his ribs.

"I told you I was in Denver that night."

"But we checked with your company. You got off work at five that day. For you to be ruled out as a suspect, we would need hard evidence of you having been in Denver. We checked the traffic cameras from the entrance ramp on I-25. There's no sign of your car entering the highway between the hours of five and seven, which puts you nowhere near Denver at the time of the shooting."

"Well, I'm not sure what to tell you. I left right after work." Connor felt a rush of adrenaline pump through his body. They were on to him, and there was no denying it at this point.

"If you'd like to cooperate with our investigation, allow us to search your apartments."

"Both of them?"

"Is that a problem?"

"No. That's fine." His mind raced. He knew his Pueblo apartment was clear of any evidence. His Denver residence, however, had his guns and ammunition, along with all the research he had done on Jeremy Heston. They would go to his Pueblo apartment first, seeing as it was the closest and more relevant. During that time he could drive to Denver and clear that apartment of any evidence. Once they checked out both homes and found nothing, he'd be able to return to a normal life.

His dream of killing Jeremy Heston had turned into a nightmare with his botched attempt. He wouldn't dare step foot on that campus ever again, and barring any setbacks on his current work project, he'd be back in Denver by summer, with no intent to ever returning to this shithole town.

"Good. We could have gotten warrants involved, but we appreciate your cooperation," the detective said sternly.

"You're welcome anytime. I don't even keep my door locked here, because I literally have nothing to steal. I've been living out of my suitcase during this project and just wanna go home when it's all done without having to pack a bunch of shit."

The detective nodded. "Great. We'll be in touch."

They had Connor fill out a form on his way out, to grant the detectives permission to search his homes. He scribbled a signature, walked calmly out of the building, then drove like hell toward Denver.

* * *

During the drive, which Connor stayed at a steady 85 miles per hour, he mentally ran through all the items he'd need to grab: the rifle, boxes of ammo, the newspaper and printed article clippings about Jeremy, and anything else that might suggest he had planned an attack on that murdering piece of shit.

Traffic was nonexistent during the middle of a weekday, and he reached his Denver residence within 90 minutes. The weather was much warmer in the city, so Connor rolled down his window to enjoy the fresh air as he pulled into his complex's parking lot. He lit a cigarette to celebrate getting away with attempted murder. The tobacco had never tasted so sweet as he held it in with each long drag, letting it coat his lungs.

He had made great time on the drive and felt confident in his plan. While those detectives had their heads up their asses in Pueblo, he'd be a couple hours ahead of them, removing all evidence that could hold up in a court of law.

Connor slammed the car door and strutted toward his apartment with his head held high, flicking away the cigarette butt. He still felt urgency in getting the task done, but knew it was best to take time so that no detail would be overlooked.

The elevator took him to the third floor. Loud, muffled music poured from the speakers of one of his neighbor's apartments, something that would have normally annoyed him, but today was a special day, so Connor bobbed his head to the beat of what sounded like hard rock.

When he reached his apartment door, he felt no resistance from the dead bolt. *Did I not lock it?* He tried to think back to the night he had returned home to drop off the rifle. His mind had been so flustered, it was possible he forgot. *But I never forget the dead bolt.*

Connor pushed the door open, and as it creaked to a halt he saw two men in suits standing in his kitchen. One held a stack of all the papers he had compiled on Jeremy Heston, and the other held his rifle in two gloved hands. The man holding the rifle grinned as a look of shock spread across Connor's face.

The feeling in Connor's legs vanished immediately as his mind told him to run. The better part of his conscience kept him in place, though; he knew running would only add to his guilt and eventual prison sentence.

"Surprised to see us, Mr. Chappell?" the man holding the rifle asked him mockingly.

What the fuck?

"I think he's surprised," said the man with the papers.

"Did you know the minimum sentence for first degree attempted murder is ten years?" asked the man holding the rifle. "Ten years at least. We have hard evidence of motive and premeditation, plus this beautiful weapon that forensics can confirm later was the gun used in your botched attempt. What do you say to that?"

Connor said nothing, his mind now stuck and unable to process how it all had snowballed out of control so fast.

"Don't get me wrong," he continued. "I hate that Heston

kid, too. I had to investigate that crime scene. Do you have any idea what thirteen dead bodies in a closed space smells like?"

Connor's mind wandered to the crime scene photos he had seen of his brother's body on the floor of the office. The thought usually led to a burst of rage, but his emotions only allowed him to stay in a panicked state.

"We have a justice system in place for a reason. No room for vigilantes taking matters into their own hands."

The man placed the firearm on Connor's counter top and approached the frozen suspect. He pulled out a pair of handcuffs.

"Connor Chappell, you're under arrest for the attempted murder of Jeremy Heston. Please turn around, don't make this any more difficult than it needs to be."

Connor turned and faced out his door toward the hallway. The man slapped the cuffs around his wrists while informing him of his rights.

How could this have happened? I thought I was home-free.

30

Chapter 30

Jeremy wished he had drugs to knock him into a deep sleep. He'd have a long night ahead and would be running on fumes—and fatigue could cause the simplest of missteps. A misstep at this point in his life could virtually end it.

He laid down on the train car's ashy floor and closed his eyes, praying to God to let him sleep for just one hour. But the excitement and adrenaline would never allow it.

His sense of time was still off, but thinking back to the moment he had burst out of the hospital like a cannon ball, he figured two hours had passed, making the time somewhere in the neighborhood of 3:30.

Jeremy had spent the last hour thinking about what a ridiculous hiding spot this was. Any police officer worth their salt would know to look in the rail yard. An asylum escapee wouldn't last long in a public neighborhood, leaving no choice but to hide in one of the hundreds of abandoned train cars. They would just take their time on their search, check out each car one by one, until they found him.

"Good try, Heston," they would say. "Nowhere for you to go now."

It was a truly chilling moment for Jeremy, more so even than the time he equipped himself in the Open Hands parking lot, knowing what lay ahead. The next twenty-four hours would essentially decide the rest of his life—the ultimate crossroads of his experiment. He'd either be caught in the train car and sent back to the hospital, where he would remain in solitary confinement until his death, or he would be free to continue his mission.

This is all for you, Damon. And at this point it was. Without Damon, Jeremy could have easily spent the next twenty years of his life waiting around like a fool, hoping for a release that would never come.

Damon had accelerated the process, taking his own life so Jeremy could continue his work. The fact that someone believed so strongly in Jeremy's vision was all he needed to keep moving forward. There would be others who felt as passionate as Damon, and he needed to reach them, let them know they were not alone.

At this moment, Jeremy started to roll around in the soot like a little kid playing in the snow. After fifteen minutes he had succeeded in covering every square inch of his body in the soot. His white uniform had turned black, not a trace of whiteness visible. His skin, from his ankles to his eyelids, were also black. Jeremy imagined that he looked like a coal miner who had just woken up from a ten-year nap in the mine.

The floor of the train car had such a thick layer of soot, it appeared untouched after Jeremy's gymnastics session.

Set yourself up for success, he thought. He'd lay flat on his back until nightfall, blending in to the blackness of the train car, praying to God that the police wouldn't see him when they peeked over the edge.

* * *

But the police never came, which made Jeremy both excited and uneasy. What reason on Earth would have prevented them from taking a look around the rail yard? Did the sound from the ground below not travel into the train car?

He supposed that was possible, as the car's soot covered walls fully engulfed him from the rest of the rail yard. The police could have been all over the yard with dogs and Jeremy might never have heard them. His blanket of coal might have also kept any dogs from sniffing him out, especially in such a large space.

When the sun set for good, Jeremy stood up, deciding it was safe, and paced laps around the train car. The cold air nipped at his bare arms and he rubbed them ferociously as he walked. He waited another hour, by his estimate, before deciding to take a look at his surroundings. It had all passed by in a blur earlier in the day, but he was thankful to have made it this far.

He climbed the interior ladder with silent steps, careful not to cause a sound that might draw attention to his location. The view from the top of the car amazed Jeremy.

Under the moonlight, he saw rows of train cars that stretched as far as he could see. He knew the rail yard was massive, as he had seen it from a slightly uphill vantage point when he arrived, but he hadn't had the chance to truly take in its grandness.

Jeremy looked left, right, backward, and forward. Abandoned train cars were everywhere. Damon had done some intensive research to conclude that this would be a reliable hideout after an escape. The image of his newest friend collapsing like a tower of Jenga blocks would likely stay burned into his memory forever. Every day of freedom that Jeremy enjoyed, Damon would remain in the forefront of his thoughts. He owed him his life, and wanted nothing more than to follow through so Damon's death wouldn't be in vain.

Jeremy crawled over the edge and descended the ladder, gravel crunching beneath his shoes as they hit the ground. No one had come looking for him, to his knowledge, and he'd have to take advantage of the night to make sure the rest of his escape plan played out according to plan.

31

Chapter 31

Jeremy wandered south in the dark, cold rail yard for ten minutes before meeting his first obstacle.

"Shit!"

The Arkansas River rippled quietly, keeping him from the other side of town. The river was about thirty feet wide. Swimming across it would be too risky, with the temperature dropping by the minute. It had been a couple of hours since the sun went down, so he estimated it to be ten o'clock.

What a laugh they'd all have if I died from hypothermia after making it this far.

Then he saw that a bridge towered a hundred feet above him, complete with a road and pedestrian walkway. He could see the soft glow of streetlights lining the path above.

Jeremy retreated back to the rail yard and climbed up the hill to where the bridge started, which turned out to be Fourth Street. He was delighted to find the pedestrian sidewalk spacious and fenced off. Any passing cars would have a hard time seeing him in the dark, especially with his all-black appearance.

He started to shiver and rubbed his arms. A long exhale

showed his breath in white clouds, and he knew he'd need to hurry before he turned into a human popsicle.

Hurry where, Jeremy? You don't have anywhere to go. You're gonna freeze to death in Pueblo, Colorado. Ever think that's how your life would end?

The bridge stretched a half-mile. Jeremy's legs already throbbed with pain after his frantic two-mile sprint from the hospital, and now he felt a stinging sensation with each step. The thought of freezing—or, worse, being caught and sent back to the hospital—kept him moving forward.

It took him fifteen minutes to cross the bridge and turn off the path into the neighborhood he had seen from the other side of the river. A few cars had zipped by him, but the bridge remained desolate. He peered back to the river below and the rail yard behind it, admiring how far he had come.

The only way to reach the finish line is one step at a time.

He made a mental note of his bearings should he have to turn and run back to the rail yard, despite the sense of ease that had settled over his nerves thanks to the quiet block of homes he walked along. The breeze picked up and howled around Jeremy, wind chimes sounding off in the distance, a dog barking.

Streetlights glowed above the row of houses he walked along when Jeremy heard a sound that made his heart freeze.

Destiny.

It was a steady sputter from a car engine that grew louder with each step. Three houses down, a black Chrysler 300 spewed exhaust, creating a thick fog in the chilled air. The headlights and internal lights were off, and Jeremy strolled cautiously next to it to confirm it was empty. He paused, feeling the warmth off the engine, and glanced around to the house that he supposed belonged to the car's owner. He noted a light flickering from the front porch, but the home appeared undisturbed otherwise.

The car's steady vibrations dared him to get in the driver's seat.

If you get in this car, they'll have something concrete to find you with. Someone will make the connection and they'll be on you like a glove.

Jeremy could drive in the opposite direction of the highway and find a small town within minutes. There were plenty of side roads that led back to Denver; he would just need a map or directions to figure out the best route. A car would also provide him with warmth overnight, an escalating concern at the moment. Where was he supposed to find clothes at this late hour? All he needed was a good hiding spot, and he could figure everything out from there.

Jeremy pulled open the Chrysler's door, the abandoned leather seat welcoming him, and sat behind the wheel.

"You picked the wrong night to warm up your car," Jeremy cackled, staring into the rearview mirror while driving away. He kept the headlights off, to remain invisible in the night. Whoever had started their car was apparently in no rush to return to it, and would be in for a big surprise when they did.

"Where to go?" Jeremy asked the empty car. A tangy smell of cleaning chemicals filled his nose. The interior was immaculate: its dashboard polished, seats vacuumed, and not one piece of trash lying around. It felt like driving a brand-new car.

The Chrysler coasted through the neighborhood, remaining silent, as Jeremy refused to touch the accelerator until he reached a main road. The car had a V8 engine, so any touch on the gas pedal would cause a roar in the quiet night.

When he reached Fourth Street, he drove two more blocks

until signs directed him to Pueblo Community College. *A college campus should have plenty of parking hideouts.*

The lights from campus glowed in the dark, providing enough visibility for Jeremy to see its parking garage. With no attendants present and the armed gate standing tall in the air, Jeremy let himself into the parking garage and drove to the bottom level underground. One other car was in the lot and he parked several spaces away from it.

"This should do," Jeremy said as he killed the engine, reclined his seat, and let sleep take control of his exhausted mind and body. His brain throbbed and itched with fatigue, and he was amazed he had made it this far without collapsing.

The clock on the dashboard read *11:52*. It had been a long, adventurous day, but finding this unattended vehicle on his first night out was a clear sign that he was on the right path to his destiny.

* * *

A slamming of car doors jolted Jeremy out of sleep the next morning.

Police! was his first thought, but once he gathered his bearings, he settled down at the sight of college students hurrying out of the lot with their backpacks slung over their shoulders.

The clock on the dashboard showed a time of *7:15*, and the morning classes appeared to be underway thanks to all the cars that now filled the garage. Cars were parked on either side of Jeremy's new Chrysler, meaning some people must have seen him sleeping behind the wheel, though that was not a particularly strange sight on a college campus.

Rays of sun peeked down the ramp from the ground-level entrance, but the garage remained mostly illuminated by its own lights. He realized, too, that all the windows had fogged up from his breathing all night. The car had remained warm enough for comfort as he slept nine hours of the deepest sleep he could remember having had in years.

Now where? he wondered as he turned on the engine. *Would they have already connected the stolen car to me? I can wait here a little longer, then try to drive out of town. Cañon City is west, Colorado Springs and Denver are north, New Mexico is south, and I have no idea what's east.*

For having spent his whole life in Colorado, Jeremy could only locate the biggest cities on a map. What he could say with confidence was that I-25 drew a clear line between two different types of people in the state. The eastern plains were home to farmers and the country lifestyle, while the western slope was home to the mountain lifestyle: ski resorts, hot springs, hiking, bike trails, and any other outdoor activity one could dream of.

City people lived near I-25, either in Denver or in one of the many surrounding suburbs. Jeremy considered the demographics of his options. While staying in a small town seemed ideal, small-town locals usually stayed in the know about area news, and were never shy to gossip about the happenings around town. Should Jeremy try to start a new life in a small town, someone would surely connect the dots and turn him in.

Wherever I go, I need a shower. He studied his arms, which still remained dark, small patches of his white skin and clothes

166

revealing themselves beneath the soot.

It seemed easier to blend in with the crowd by going back to Denver. There was a higher presence of police, and people in general, who might recognize him, but he'd be less likely to be noticed. Walking around downtown Denver on a weekday would look less suspicious than a stroll around Cañon City, where people would talk about the strange new guy in town. In Denver, people were too consumed with their own lives to worry about the random stranger on the bus.

"I'm coming home," Jeremy said with a smirk.

Damon had thought many details over when devising an escape plan, but the small town versus big city debate might have been one he overlooked. "You may need to live on the streets for a bit," Damon had told him. Jeremy remembered those words, and the way his stomach sunk when hearing them. Jeremy knew he wasn't cut out for life on the streets, especially after nearly three years of being institutionalized.

When I get to Denver, then what? Jeremy asked himself. He needed to start thinking like a detective. Were they even looking for him? *I'm Jeremy Heston, the most infamous person in Colorado.* He knew there was no chance they'd just let him go. News of his escape would have caused an uproar, especially back in Denver where the survivors and family members lived.

News. If he could find a news outlet, there would certainly be stories covering his escape. They might even mention what happened to Damon, a question that had gnawed at Jeremy since he watched the emergency exit door close behind him at the hospital. *A library should be safe, one in the suburbs. But I have to get cleaned up first.*

Jeremy debated whether he should try to contact his parents. He wanted to know why they had never come to visit, although now the answer seemed obvious. They were done with him, but if he could just explain everything like he should've the night before the shooting, then maybe they would open their hearts to him again. Would they help him live a life undercover? The thought had been throbbing in his subconscious ever since he found out he'd have the opportunity to escape. He also remembered Damon's warning not to contact anyone from his old life.

He couldn't hold on to the car for long. He'd have to ditch it soon after returning to Denver, and he'd need to leave it somewhere far from where he planned on staying.

Was there anyone at all who would take him in? He pondered this over but could only think of his uncle Ricky as a possibility. They hadn't seen each other since the trial, but Jeremy thought he might open his home to him. It was hard to know for sure how his uncle might react.

"Uncle Ricky, I hope you're ready, because Jeremy's coming home!" he shouted in the car and howled in laughter. The sense of freedom took hold of his mind and he felt like a little kid running circles in a big park: energetic and without a care in the world.

32

Chapter 32

As Jeremy approached the entrance to I-25 an hour later, a voice in his head talked him out of it. "Frontage road it is," he said as he passed the on-ramp, taking the next left instead. He knew of one frontage road that ran along the freeway from Pueblo to the heart of Colorado Springs. From there, he continued on a different frontage road, but this part of the route broke into different sections. Some stretches would take him a couple miles east of the highway, only to have him have to drive back west to find the continuation of the frontage road.

He drove this way for an hour before arriving in Castle Rock, an hour south of downtown Denver. From Castle Rock, Jeremy had no other choice but to take I-25. Once he got closer to the city, he could take the side roads to Ricky's house in Buckley, a Denver suburb only twenty minutes north of Castle Rock.

Jeremy's stomach growled angrily, but he ignored it and kept his concentration on the road and the rearview mirror, praying to God that a cop car wouldn't appear.

* * *

Twenty minutes later Jeremy arrived in Buckley, with no trace of the police in his rearview. The sensation of being followed had grown with every mile, but he knew they wouldn't simply follow him quietly. They would restrain him at the first opportunity they had—so he dismissed the feeling as paranoia. He drove another ten minutes to his uncle's home, where he hadn't been in three years. Jeremy barely remembered which streets to turn on, but once he arrived in the neighborhood it all came flooding back.

His uncle's house was in a small cul-de-sac, surrounded by three other homes and a pathway that led to a community park. Jeremy had never met the neighbors, but according to Uncle Ricky they always kept to themselves.

Jeremy parked the Chrysler at the sidewalk and killed the engine. His uncle's car wasn't parked in the driveway like it usually was. If Ricky wasn't home, that might be for the best. Jeremy knew where he kept a spare key along the side of the house; he could let himself in. Next to the front door, Jeremy looked through a window into the main dining room and saw that all the lights were off. It was nearing noon, and Ricky normally worked from home. He could have been out of town, though, or at his cabin, oblivious to the target practice Jeremy had done before the shooting.

What if he's at the police station being questioned about me? It's no secret we were close, they could already be on my tail.

The paranoia won and Jeremy returned to his car and drove it four blocks away, on the other side of the park behind his uncle's house. This allowed him to approach his uncle's house from the backyard, remaining out of sight for the most part.

He could take his time letting himself in.

Jeremy ran through all the possibilities as he walked across the park. He thought of a homemade sandwich and soda, but forced himself to walk calmly through the park.

He had sweat oozing from his pores. His shirt clung to his back, reminding him that he would also need a change of clothes, along with a much-needed shower. *Clothes, food, and money,* he thought, adding it to his mental checklist. *Get those three things and I'm ready to go.*

When he arrived at Ricky's house, he hopped the back fence and tiptoed to the side of the house where the key was hidden. A standard brick was stuffed into the dirt to the right of the garage's side door. Jeremy brushed the dirt off the brick and pulled it out, revealing a small compartment on the underside where the key waited.

"Thank you for being so forgetful," Jeremy said as he jiggled the key in the door. Uncle Ricky liked to go on walks around the park and would often forget to take his house key. After he had first moved into this house two decades ago, Jeremy could remember making the drive from Larkwood to Buckley with his mom to let Ricky back in his house. Three of those trips finally pushed Ricky to get the hidden key, vowing to never be locked out of his own house again.

The door swung open to reveal an empty garage. His uncle had a work table and tool boxes that surrounded the perimeter. Posters of exotic women in exotic places decorated the walls, while everything else remained immaculate. Jeremy had never understood why Ricky parked his car outside of the garage when he clearly had the space for it inside.

Two small steps connected the garage to the house, the entryway a small mud room that led to the living room. Jeremy put the key into this door and swung it open to a blast of warmth radiating from the central heating system.

Ricky was clearly gone. The coat rack that welcomed Jeremy was bare, the shoe mat on the ground vacant, and there was an overall sense that this home hadn't seen life in it for at least a few days.

Jeremy let the heavy door swing shut behind him and proceeded into the living room, where two couches faced a television mounted on the wall. The house reeked of citrus cleaning chemicals. He could see the park out of the living room's only window, which spanned the length of the room.

Jeremy crossed into the kitchen and noticed a note on the counter.

Rosita,

Please clean the oven this week, I made a mess :)

See you next week!

Ricky

"Rosita?" Jeremy asked the empty house. "Does he have a cleaning lady?" Jeremy assumed so, figuring his uncle had more decency than to leave a note like that for a girlfriend. This explained the citrus scent that filled the house.

More important was the "See you next week!" Ricky was certainly out of town. Jeremy didn't know what day it was. He found a calendar on the wall that was of no help, as he realized he didn't know the date either.

He crossed back to the living room and turned the TV to

a local news station. It was lunchtime, and finding a local channel showing anything besides court TV or soap operas proved difficult.

"So it's a weekday for sure," Jeremy said before flipping the channel to a network news station.

The sight of his face on the TV sunk his heart into the deepest depths of his soul. His mugshot split the screen, along with his patient portrait from the hospital. The world around him came to a standstill as the news analyst spoke about him in a droning voice.

"He escaped the mental asylum two days ago and is considered armed and dangerous," the analyst said.

Armed? I don't have a gun.

"If you see him, do not approach and call 9-1-1 immediately."

Bunch of propaganda to scare people.

The images of his face that filled the screen disappeared and gave way to a panel of three broadcasters. The headline on the bottom of the screen read: OPEN HANDS OFFICE SHOOTER ON THE RUN.

On the left of the screen, a young black man with a deep voice spoke first. "Jeremy Heston is a danger to himself and others. Here we have a young man with nothing to lose. A young man who has spent the last two years of his life in jail, court, and the mental hospital. A young man who slaughtered thirteen of his coworkers. I'm sick and tired of political correctness, let's call him what he really is: a terrorist!"

"I don't normally agree with the labeling, Darius, but you raise a good point," the middle-age blond woman in the middle said. "Terrorists are smart, calculating, and cool under pressure. I'd say these words also describe Jeremy Heston. The city of Denver needs to be on high alert. I fully expect he's in a hideout right now, plotting his next move. This is a mentally unhinged man, so there's no saying how this will end up, but I pray the authorities find him and return him to the hospital."

The man on the right, much older than his two counterparts, spoke, and his voice was the one Jeremy had heard when his face had filled the screen.

"We have a mental health issue in this country. We also have a gun issue," the man said calmly. "I wish it hadn't become such a polarizing debate, where people feel they have to pick a side. To the viewers out there, please know this is not the case. It's okay for you to acknowledge that both issues are serious matters for our country. I'd say the fear and uncertainty around Jeremy Heston being back out in the public shows that our gun problem might be the bigger matter to tackle first."

The two other analysts nodded in agreement as Jeremy watched in amazement.

He continued, "If guns weren't an issue, I promise you there would be less fear right now. Mentally ill people roam society every day, undiagnosed, and practically all of them are no harm to society. Every once in a while we get someone like Jeremy Heston who raises the stakes by getting a gun."

"Not just a gun, a semi-automatic killing machine," the blond chimed in.

"Exactly. Imagine a world where citizens didn't have access to these kinds of weapons. You actually don't have to imagine it—go to Japan, the UK, or Australia to see for yourself. But imagine if Jeremy Heston escaped a mental hospital there. Would there be widespread panic across the city and country? Probably not, because the citizens would know he has no access to modern weaponry and is really only a threat in a fistfight."

Jeremy shook his head, disgusted. The point of all of this was to start a debate on mental illness, not to further the push against guns.

"We don't have that luxury," the analyst said. "We live in a country that has mass shootings every week. We live in a country where 33,000 people die every year from gunshots. That's equivalent to the amount of deaths during the entire Korean War."

Jeremy felt two inches tall. How could he have gone through all of this planning and sacrifice, just to see the same old debate that happened after every mass shooting? His was supposed to be different, because he didn't blast his own head off and chose to face the music in court. To top it all off, he'd actually succeeded in his goal of escaping a criminal sentence and being sent to the mental hospital. Everything was in place, but these dumb fucks on the news wanted to blame guns.

If he flipped the channel to the network's main competitor, he'd find nothing but NRA propaganda arguing why we needed more guns. A sinking feeling crept into Jeremy and he wasn't sure if it was defeat, embarrassment, or regret.

For the first time in two years, Jeremy truly doubted his experiment. All it took was two minutes in front of a TV to know that nothing would ever change. Society was doomed to debate this topic of mental health and guns for eternity, or until *everyone* was killed by a lunatic with a gun.

"Wasteful. I did all this to get mental health in the limelight, but no one cares. No one's talking about mental health."

Calm down. This is one channel and three people's opinion. Your work isn't done. Do your due diligence and find out how society really feels.

"They don't care. They don't give a shit." Jeremy started to cry. He would search online to see what people really thought of him. Social media was always crawling with opinions and that would be a perfect gauge for how the people felt. If some defended him in the name of mental health, then he would know this was not a lost cause. If everyone was opposed, however, and only wanted to talk about guns or locking him in prison, then that would settle the score.

Jeremy turned off the TV, not wanting to hear any more of the bullshit.

"Slow down and think. You have time. Ricky is gone for a few days."

Shit, what day is it? Jeremy had forgotten why he had turned the TV on in the first place.

"Fuck it, I'm getting on the Internet."

He threw the remote on the couch and stormed to his uncle's office upstairs, pounding the stairs with each step he took, black dust covering the recently cleaned carpet.

Chapter 33

Jeremy wasted no time once he sat at his uncle's computer desk. As the computer fired up, he admired the wide collection of Denver sports memorabilia decorating the walls of the immaculate office.

A quick search returned stunning results. Jeremy typed his name into Google and received 135,000,000 results. The first page was splayed with his face, images from jail, the hospital, the court room, and even his college ID photo. The right-hand panel showed his date of birth, height, nationality, education, and parents' names. Below this information was the "People also search for..." box that showed the names and faces of some of the most notorious mass murderers in recent American history.

The first link on the search results took him to his own Wikipedia page, an informational site that shared every detail of his life. Reading about his history on such a famous site sent chills down his spine.

You know you've made it big when Wikipedia gives you a page.

A quick sift through the first twenty pages of results contained everything from news reports from every outlet imaginable, opinion editorials, YouTube videos, and social media groups that had sprouted up because of him.

Jeremy lost himself for the next three hours, reading article after article, watching video clips of him in court, and other clips similar to the one he had just caught on live television. It was an out-of-body experience he didn't want to end.

"I have fans," he said, taken aback at the fact.

One link led him to a Facebook page called Heston's Homies, where people actually defended him, some on the basis of mental illness, but the majority out of a strange, twisted love for him. Teenage girls had posted sickening photos with his face edited into portraits with them, and some posted photos of what they thought their future kids would look like with Jeremy as the father.

"You can open your hands to me, Jeremy!" one girl had posted, referencing his former company's name. There were thousands of posts on this fan page. Jeremy scrolled through them, feeling more disgusted with each passing minute.

"This wasn't the point. I didn't do this for fame."

The articles regarding his mental state and how mental illness had caused his actions were few and far between. The ones he came across were well written, intelligent, and deliberate in delivering the message he wanted, as if he had written it up himself. Unfortunately, these articles were buried under a heap of shit made up of gun control, fan girls, and useless opinions from random strangers with a blog.

Even with the insanity verdict, the public seemed to grow more outraged with the country's legal system, claiming it was too soft on "monsters" like Jeremy.

He had super fans, but Jeremy had at least 100 times more people who wanted him dead. They believed people like him didn't deserve hope and should rot in a jail cell until death, or be killed by lethal injection. A coalition had formed to hunt him down after his escape—a group who called themselves the Warriors for Justice promised they would find Jeremy, wherever he was, and "put thirteen slugs into his useless body," since the courts didn't want to do the right thing.

This didn't faze Jeremy; he wouldn't be caught. If the police couldn't find him, how would some tough guy behind a keyboard be able to locate and kill him?

It did, however, remind Jeremy to search for his old friend, Damon, and see what exactly the hell had happened when he had collapsed to the floor. It felt like five years ago, when in reality it was only three days. He changed his search to JEREMY HESTON ESCAPE.

The results brought back exactly what he wanted. The *Washington Post* had done a detailed timeline of events of that day, trying to see how it all could have gone so wrong for the hospital. Was it a planned escape or was it pure luck?

They started with breakfast, taking the reader through a day in the life of a mental patient. He skimmed over this to get to the good part. Lunch had ended shortly after one. At this point, a nurse recalled seeing Damon stand up from his table where he had sat alone, looking queasy. The nurse approached him, calling out to him and getting no response. Damon collapsed to the floor, spreading instant panic.

The seconds following this were critical. Since no one at the hospital could piece together an actual timeline, they used the security footage that showed Jeremy bolting down the hallway toward the exit, within seconds of Damon becoming the focus of everyone's attention. The footage followed Jeremy outside and around a building, where he hopped the fence and vanished into the fields.

"He appeared to have a clear-cut plan, like he knew exactly where to run," Dr. Garza was quoted as saying. "I believe this was planned, with our deceased patient, as a way for Mr. Heston to escape. We're just not sure why Damon would have done something so drastic for someone he only met a couple of months ago, and now we'll never know."

Jeremy read on to find that Damon had overdosed on the drugs provided by the hospital, and his heart ached at the thought. They had only met a couple months prior, but Damon was a believer, and knew Jeremy could do big things for the mental health movement. If only Damon could've known how Jeremy was already perceived in the public eye, he might have reconsidered.

"None of these people are going to read a book written by me, or listen to anything I have to say. They hate me."

What did you expect, dumbass? You killed innocent people for no reason, at least in their eyes.

Jeremy found it impossible to stop clicking on different articles. The final link he clicked on set off a rage of fury he had not felt in years.

"Motherfucker, you're kidding me!" Jeremy barked. The mouse trembled in his hand, blood feeling like it might explode out of his veins, as he scrolled through the article, finding a blog post titled *Jeremy Heston: The Lies Behind Mental Illness.*

The blog was a 30-page post written about Jeremy's extensive trial process. It included excerpts of witness testimony, quotes from jurors, attorneys, judges, doctors, and basically anyone involved in the legal process. The author mentioned a full book on the matter was due to come out the following year. The content all boiled down to one conclusion: Jeremy Heston's insanity defense was a crock of shit. The author claimed that Jeremy's doctor and defense team were part of a conspiracy to fudge the facts to make Jeremy appear more insane than he really was. He claimed the family's mental illness genetics to be a hoax.

It wasn't so much the ridiculous claims made by the blog's author that boiled Jeremy's blood, but rather the author himself.

That sore loser beat me to the punch.

Jeremy closed the Internet browser after reading the author page: former Denver District Attorney Geoffrey Batchelor.

34

Chapter 34

The hot water filled the bathroom with steam, fogging the window and mirrors. Jeremy stepped into the shower and let the water flow over his body, the black crud that had coated him washing away and swirling down the drain. He couldn't remember the last time he'd taken a shower in private, and he relished the white noise of running water to help clear his mind.

His hands still trembled in rage and he felt he might vomit when he thought of Geoff Batchelor's blog post. It had been released only three months after the verdict, meaning the DA had to have started writing it almost right away. Jeremy battled with what his next move should be as he rubbed the bar of soap across his crusty skin.

I can turn myself in, go back to the hospital, and spend the rest of my life there living a fairly happy life. I can stay on the run and live every day in fear of being caught. I can flee to Mexico or Canada and start over where nobody will know me. I can still try to write my book, give secret talks to my apparent fan base, and try to rise as a warrior for mental health. Will they give me a free pass if they see I'm doing good work? Or will they still fight to capture and detain me no matter how harmless I become?

I could assassinate Geoff Batchelor for single-handedly ruining my plan with his stupid blog of lies.

You know what to do next. Don't act like you haven't thought about Ricky's rifle hiding away in his closet. The crazy guy in the suit already told you what you're gonna do. Get back out there and give the world what they expect from you, Mr. Armed and Dangerous.

Jeremy felt hope slipping away by the second. All this planning, all the preparation for this moment was already becoming a moot point because of people like Geoff Batchelor, standing in the corner waiting to call bullshit on anything that didn't fit their closed-minded agenda.

"Fuck him. Fuck them all."

* * *

After a thirty-minute shower, Jeremy dried himself off and slipped on a pair of sweatpants and a T-shirt from his uncle's closet. His dark hair was slicked back as he let it dry naturally. His skin was white again and he disposed of his hospital uniform in the trash can in the garage. After the shower, Jeremy's body begged for sleep, still trying to catch up from the emotional roller coaster of the last 48 hours.

What about the car? It hadn't come up in any of the searches or news reports. The stolen car hadn't even been mentioned. Did they not think it was connected? Did they not want Jeremy to know they were on to him? Did the car's owner even report the car as missing? He looked out the back window across the park and wondered if the car was still parked where he had left it.

He pushed it to the back of his mind to focus on the task at hand.

The thought of killing the old DA excited Jeremy (it always had), but he quickly dismissed it. With Geoff on the campaign trail for governor, he likely had a security team around at all times in public. They wouldn't take too kind to an assassination attempt and Jeremy could very well find himself on the wrong end of a bullet. He'd gone through it once and didn't want to find out how much worse it could end.

That damned man in the suit also kept creeping into his mind. He had called Jeremy a killer, twice, and now he was starting to believe it. Why else would his fate have brought him to this point? Was his original plan a bit ambitious? Sure, but he'd pulled it off. He'd killed thirteen people and managed to only spend time in jail during the trial. Then, after a few months in a mental hospital, he actually escaped, and hadn't been caught after two days on the run. The odds of those events ever happening to one person again had to be like a person winning the lottery and being struck by lightning in the same day.

"First things first," Jeremy said as he paced around the living room, fighting off the urge to sleep. Pacing circles had become a habit, to get his creative juices flowing.

He ran back up the stairs, this time not outraged but rather inspired, and let himself into his uncle's bedroom. The room smelled like freshly cleaned laundry as the dim sunlight tried to claw its way through the dark curtains.

Jeremy crossed the room to the closet, slid open the door, and rummaged through a pile of dirty clothes. Clearly the cleaning lady had no interest in doing his laundry. Behind the pile, Jeremy pulled out a silver alloy case, which he dropped gently on the bed.

There were no locks, for his uncle believed what waited inside should be easily accessible in case of an emergency. He flipped up the latches, allowing the lid to pop open. Jeremy lifted the lid all the way to reveal an M-16, the assault rifle he had first fired at the shooting range with his uncle many years ago.

"Hello, old friend."

If this isn't your destiny, I'm not sure what is, Jeremy's mind reminded him as he pulled the gun out of the case, revealing packs of ammunition below it. A quick mental count calculated roughly 200 total rounds available for use, along with a handful of magazines. His heart throbbed excitedly at the sight of everything in the case.

Jeremy smiled. "Everything I need is here. Now all I need is a plan." The thought took his mind to his coveted notebook, by now a likely rotting corpse of once-meaningful pages sitting in a landfill, containing the truth behind everything he had done for the last two years.

This time around would be different. Jeremy didn't need to maintain a secret life while planning a mass murder. All he needed to do was stay out of the public eye and come up with a game plan that could be easily executed.

Two hundred rounds and a fully automatic weapon gave him endless possibilities.

"Think public gatherings. Festivals at the park. Downtown on a weekend. Movie theaters, churches, concerts. Take your pick, the world is yours."

Two years ago, Jeremy had reached a point in the planning where it felt like an evil alter ego had taken control of the wheel and had driven him through to the finish line. Today, standing in his uncle's empty bedroom with an automatic weapon, that voice inside returned.

Am I insane?

"Insane people aren't capable of planning things like this, or of diagnosing themselves. Remember?"

It had been awhile since he had a full conversation with himself, but for old time's sake, why not?

"You tried to do society a service. You tried to bridge the gap for the mentally ill and the general public."

And what did they do?

"They spit on your name and your work. Some hated you, some glorified you, but none of it was about mental health."

You failed, Jeremy. Just admit it and move on. Get your revenge on them. Show them the truth. Maybe the second time's the charm?

Jeremy chuckled. "Not likely."

You never mentioned Jamie. Why not go find her and ask her to run away with you? Maybe she's a Heston Homie.

"Good one. She's probably left town with everyone else. I'm not talking to anyone from my past. That will only end badly."

Jeremy had lost the battle. Somehow Geoff Batchelor had pulled out the win, whether on purpose or not, and Jeremy was back to square one. He thought back to the summer of 2015, when he had first started having the initial thoughts of his plan.

"What if I had just left it as thoughts? Crazy thoughts that stayed in my head and went to the imaginary junkyard where bad ideas go? What if I never wrote it down in a notebook? What if I had gone to work on March 11 and just gone home that night and started looking for a new job? What if I opened my private practice, with Dr. Siva as my guide? Would I be effecting actual change today, or would I still be hating my job until I retired in forty years?"

It's too late for that, my friend. There's only three ways this ends for you now, just like during the trial: life in prison, life in the loony bin, or death.

35

Chapter 35

Jeremy returned to the computer and ran a search for upcoming events in the Denver area. There were basketball and hockey games, concerts, and comedy shows. The one that caught his eye, though, was an event called the Taste of Denver.

The Taste of Denver was an annual event held at downtown's Civic Center Park, where food vendors from around the city set up their food trucks for the thousands of hungry people in attendance. It ran all day, with no true peak hours, as it was a constant flood of attendees.

"Easy," Jeremy said. And it would be. He wouldn't be able to walk in the front gates with an M-16 in hand, but the park's location provided plenty of surrounding areas where he could hide and shoot from an elevated position.

The event was a weekend long, running from March 23–25, and this made Jeremy giggle. "March must be my month."

Jeremy found a pair of headphones in his uncle's desk drawer, slid them over his head, and started playing music from the computer. Techno music was his first choice, something he hadn't listened to since his teenage years, yet felt so right in the moment. The electronic sounds filled his mind with euphoria, not having heard music in nearly two years. It felt like a coating of joy spreading over his brain, firing neurons that had fallen dormant after so long.

"Music is one thing that affects the entire mind," one of his professors had once explained. "Why mental patients aren't granted full access to music is beyond me."

Jeremy had never tested this theory for himself, but this reintroduction had his mind doing cartwheels. He closed the search windows for a moment and lay on the floor to close his eyes and truly soak in the music. Despite the rapid and chaotic beat, it relaxed him. He felt home again and ready to take the next step in life.

"If I die, let them remember me forever as the first one to try." Jeremy had come to peace with the real and disturbing possibilities that awaited him. Even if he chose to not move forward with another attack on innocent lives, the chances remained that he would eventually get caught and sent back to the loony bin, or jail, or be shot by one of the vigilantes trying to hunt him like a wild animal.

The techno faded out and the next song lulled Jeremy into a deeper sense of peace. Blue Öyster Cult came on with a familiar guitar chord, right before Buck Dharma started singing to Jeremy to not fear the reaper. Jeremy felt the words flow from the headphones and throughout his body.

Death really isn't something to be afraid of, it's a real possibility every single day that most people don't take the time to appreciate. You might think you're keeping death in check by living life to the fullest, but it's always waiting in the shadows of your soul.

* * *

After Jeremy finished his personal concert in Uncle Ricky's office, he returned to trying to figure out a basic plan of attack. He searched images of past Taste of Denver events, along with the satellite map of the area around the park. He found many spots where he could post up; however, few provided him the elevated ground he would need.

He could stand on the steps of the capitol building across the street, but that place would be swarmed with police and he'd have no chance of clearing all 200 rounds of ammunition before becoming a human shooting target.

The images of the event showed a glimpse of the entrance, with its long lines stretching a block down.

"I could just come up to the line and start firing. Security will be heavy, but not on the outside." A contracted security team manned the entrance, while police patrolled inside the event. "That could work."

But you need to make this count. It's your comeback party. What happens when the 200 rounds run out? Are you gonna place your gun on the ground and wait to be arrested again like a pussy, or are you gonna make a run for it?

"They called me a terrorist, how would a terrorist get maximum casualties?"

After researching the mass shootings that had taken place since Jeremy was arrested, he came to find that the death tolls seemingly grew higher and higher with each shooting. At the time of Jeremy's shooting in March 2016, it was the fourth highest in terms of victim count: 35 total people killed or wounded. By the time Jeremy ran his search on recent shootings, he found his had fallen out of the top ten. In two years.

Think outside the box. You'll have all those people standing on a street corner. A street—

"I can drive a car through the line, through the entrance, and then open fire once inside."

Now we're talking.

"I'll certainly die. Police will shoot me on the spot."

Then you die. You've already come to terms with it. It can't be worse than spending the next forty years of your life in the same room staring at the goddamn wall.

"It could work." Jeremy closed his eyes and tried to imagine running over the line of people. Would their bodies crunch underneath the car? Would there be dents and a broken windshield to account for? Could the car get stuck in a pile of dead bodies, so that he wouldn't make it inside the festival?

There were logistics beyond his knowledge to consider, and quite frankly, he didn't have the energy to do thorough re-search again. Jeremy wanted something quick and simple that he could roll out of bed and execute on a Saturday afternoon and be done with.

"I could just snatch a car again and try it. If I get stuck, I'll just get out and start shooting."

A booming knock came from the front door and Jeremy felt his heart leap to his throat.

"Who the fuck?" he whispered, and crossed the upstairs hallway from the office into his uncle's bedroom.

Jeremy peeked through the side of the curtain and saw a cop car outside the house.

"Fuck, fuck, fuck!"

Hide. Relax.

"They know I'm here. They're watching the Internet

searches and know it's me. They know Ricky's gone." Paranoid thoughts raced in circles like a hamster wheel in Jeremy's mind.

Calm down. They don't know shit. Hide.

Jeremy paced in circles around his uncle's bedroom. "Where the fuck am I going to hide?"

The bed was massive, a California king, and the room was dim. Underneath the bed seemed as good a place as any, so Jeremy dropped to the ground as another thunderous knock echoed throughout the house, his heart pounding against his rib cage to match the sound.

He slithered like a snake until the pressure of the box spring above pushed down on his body. His eyes, arms, and fingers all throbbed simultaneously with adrenaline.

Another knock came, and Jeremy clenched his hands into fists and closed his eyes, praying they would go away.

* * *

When the knocking ended and the engine outside revved up, Jeremy let out a long sigh as the trembling left his body.

"Okay, so they don't think I'm here, or they would have broken down the door."

But they're on to you. Why else would they be knocking on your uncle's door on a random weekday afternoon?

Jeremy needed to hang low for a couple more days inside the house. There might be surveillance set up on the house and he couldn't risk being caught.

There was enough food to last a few more days, but his uncle would certainly notice all of his snacks missing. The date was

March 21, but the Taste of Denver festival didn't start until March 23.

"How long can I chance staying here until he comes home? What would he do if he came home and found me? Call the cops? Help me hide?"

Jeremy believed his uncle would help him hide. Wasn't family supposed to be supportive no matter what? He could live the rest of his life hiding in his uncle's basement, but was that any better than the alternatives?

Jeremy had grown antsy during his stay in the hospital. Once he stopped taking the medication, he felt a sense of urgency to do *something*. Sitting in the same room every day took a toll on an active mind like his, and now that he was out, he still couldn't do whatever he wanted.

"A prison without bars," he groaned.

Move tomorrow. Hide somewhere. The weather is decent, you'll be fine. But leave this house exactly as you found it.

Jeremy agreed with his inner voice. "One more day. I'll stay tonight and tomorrow, and leave tomorrow night. Moving in the night will be much easier."

He'd pushed the plan for the festival attack to the back of his mind, but had every intention of seeing it through—preferably on its busiest day, Saturday. The M-16 would be difficult to tote around town, so he'd need to find a location where he could blend in and hide the weapon.

Working his way toward downtown would be best. There were swarms of homeless people he could hide among. Driving the car would be risky, but not as risky as getting on a train, bus, or cab with an assault rifle slung around his shoulder. The car was his only viable option. Once he arrived downtown, he could ditch the car for good.

You need to sleep as much as you can tonight and tomorrow, because the following three days are going to be a shit show.

Jeremy ate some cookies with a glass of milk, before returning to the computer to scout out a potential spot to stay downtown.

There were plenty to choose from, and he figured staying near a homeless shelter would provide him the most cover. His uncle had a closet full of heavy jackets, gloves, and beanies that he planned to borrow to improve his disguise. Just because they were homeless didn't mean they wouldn't recognize his face. Famous was famous, and Jeremy couldn't risk being ratted out or murdered by a bum.

His search led him to a park five blocks north of Civic Center Park. It was a small park, but in the heart of downtown, where he knew some of the homeless population spent their nights. The park appeared to have benches and several trees to provide coverage.

He stayed on the computer until four in the afternoon before calling it quits. A good enough plan was in place, and it was time to prepare for the following night. After a quick rummage through his uncle's closet, garage, and basement, Jeremy found what he had hoped to find: a hunting backpack.

The backpack didn't only provide Jeremy a place to store the rifle instead of toting it around on his shoulder, it also added to his disguise as a homeless man. He had often seen homeless people with large backpacks stuffed with their life's belongings.

Jeremy took the oversize backpack upstairs to his uncle's room and threw it on the bed. He jammed the rifle into the backpack and found that the end of the barrel stuck out by a foot. The M-16 was more than three feet long, and the backpack would only cover two feet.

Wrap the end of it with clothes.

Jeremy nodded at this thought and stuffed the loaded magazines and extra boxes of ammunition on the bottom of the backpack, followed by layers of clothing he would need to carry, wrapping a sweater around the rifle's barrel.

"That should do it," he said. The camouflage backpack looked like it might explode, stretched to its limits. The sweater-wrapped rifle stuck out of the top and he managed to zip the bag shut right up to it. All that mattered was that the sweater hid the obvious shape of what it concealed, and Jeremy was pleased to see it had done the job.

With the bag packed, he laid out an outfit of sweatpants, a jacket, and a black beanie to travel in tomorrow night. The jacket zipped up to his nose, perfect for hiding his face in public.

The police were obviously on the lookout for him, but he felt confident that he could get around town in his disguise on Thursday and Friday, before the festival.

He crossed his arms and admired the backpack once more. It was a quickly thrown together plan, nothing near the level of detail he had completed the last time. But he felt proud just the same. Being spontaneous felt freeing, and Jeremy, who had once been terrified of the unknown, now found he loved the thought of not knowing how everything would play out.

Not like any of this worked when I had a plan to begin with, he thought. *All of those lives can't be wasted in vain. You still can succeed with your original goal. Show the world they were wrong about you.*

36

Chapter 36

Friday, Ricky sat inside his cabin, drinking a glass of scotch with his neighbor, Travis Wells. The two had just finished a steak dinner and sat at the kitchen table overlooking the mountain.

"I don't know what to do," Ricky said, taking a sip. "The whole thing makes me sick."

Ricky had just informed Travis that he found a spent bullet casing on the property and knew it had come from Jeremy. He asked Travis if he had seen anyone come to the cabin at any point in time in the months leading up to Jeremy's killing spree. His neighbor, unfortunately, hadn't spent any time at his cabin during the winter months.

"There's nothing to do. It's all over." Travis scratched his head through a forest of black hair, clearly in angst.

"But he's out again. What if he tries to come back here as a hideout? I could at least tell the police to keep an eye out."

"You could, but do you really think he'll come this far?"

"No. You're probably right."

"You have nothing to be afraid of."

"The only thing I'm afraid of is that if I ever see him, I'm gonna beat the shit out of him," Ricky said before taking a swig from the glass. "I just feel dirty living with such a secret. I should have said something during the trial. But when I looked Jeremy in the eyes from the witness stand, I could still see my nephew. My nephew who has basically been a son to me. But now, knowing he might be planning something new, I feel guilty. I could've probably put him in prison for life."

"How would it change anything?"

"It proves he planned his attack. Go look at the hundreds of bullet holes in my trees. I never shoot from right in front of the cabin, I go deep into the woods."

Ricky's cell phone buzzed on the table with an incoming call from an unknown number.

"Hello?"

"Hello, is this Mr. Richard Heston?" a stern, baritone voice asked.

"Yes, sir, who is this?"

"Good afternoon, Mr. Heston, this is Officer Reeves from the Denver Police Department. I was calling because we stopped by your house yesterday, but you weren't home."

"I'm at my cabin in the mountains. Is everything okay?" Ricky stood up from the table.

"We have reason to believe your nephew, Jeremy, may have made it back to the Denver area. Has he attempted to contact you?"

"No, sir. I've been up at my cabin for the past few days. Heard about his break-out while I was up here, in fact—but no, he has not contacted me."

"Very well, Mr. Heston. We're just covering our bases. Please get in touch right away if you spot him or hear from him."

"Is he dangerous?"

"We don't believe so. At this point, he's more of a threat to himself than others. We just put word out through the media that he is dangerous so that people will be on high alert. He'll have no access to guns, through legal means anyway."

"I see."

"Nothing to worry about, just taking precautions. I'll let you get back to your day. Thanks for your time."

The officer hung up, leaving Ricky uneasy. Travis stared at him with curious eyes, having heard half of the conversation.

"That was Denver PD. They said Jeremy may be back in Denver."

Travis shook his head. "How could he have managed to get that far from Pueblo? His face is literally all over the news, probably even more so up there."

"He's always been a sneaky bastard. Smart as hell. They told me to be on the lookout in case he tries to show up at my house."

"Or here. If he got to Denver in a couple days, he could get here no problem."

"That's true—he's probably more likely to come here than my house. This place is hidden. I should probably stay up here a little longer, just to be sure."

"Where could he go in Denver? Didn't you say your brother moved to Arizona?"

"Yeah. I'm the closest relative he has in town. We have some distant cousins, not sure if he'd even remember them. I'm not sure about his circle of friends."

"If he wanted to come here, he would've just come straight here, don't you think?"

Ricky nodded and rubbed his bald head. "I suppose that makes sense."

"If he went to your house, would he have a way in?"

Ricky pushed his glass aside and nodded slowly. "Yes. He would know how to get in." Ricky paused and stared at the bottle of scotch, debated pouring another glass. Travis watched him intently, and tilted his glass to finish the drink.

"I need to go," Ricky said. "Right now."

* * *

Ricky drove like a maniac. He had chugged two glasses of water to try and sober up before jumping into his truck and hitting the road. He shouldn't have been driving, legally speaking, but he felt he had to get to his house in Buckley as quickly as possible.

His gut feeling was that Jeremy was at his house. He could've called the police and told them about the spare key, and asked them to take a look around the house, but he wanted to bust Jeremy himself. He would still call the police if he found his nephew, but he wanted to give him a piece of his mind first.

Ricky typically used the two-hour drive from the cabin to daydream, but this trip was filled with racing thoughts of his nephew.

He wondered where it had all gone wrong for Jeremy. He'd always seemed genuinely happy every time they saw each other. Ricky found it impossible to believe Jeremy had taken such a drastic turn, to act out in such a violent manner.

Was there anything I could've done? Ricky asked himself this question every day. He tried to not beat himself up over it. If he hadn't been on the road so much, if he'd had even one or two visits with Jeremy in the months leading up to the tragedy, he wondered if it could have been prevented.

Ricky felt for the victims and survivors, but it was also true that being related to a mass murder had absolutely fucked with his psyche, and he feared it might be something he'd never recover from. No one in the family had known the thoughts going through Jeremy's mind. Nobody had seen any signs pointing to this sort of mental breakdown. Family has a way of running on autopilot, going through the motions.

Ricky thought Jeremy would have confided in him if anything was wrong. They'd had plenty of conversations about life; it wasn't always just about sports and entertainment. Had he not been as accessible as he had believed?

It doesn't matter now, it's too late for the blame game. Jeremy took those lives, not you.

* * *

After a two-hour wrestling match in his own mind, Ricky arrived home. He parked his truck in the driveway and opened the garage. He liked to keep his truck outside with the windows cracked on warm days; keeping it in the garage gave it a musty feel he didn't like.

He had packed one oversize duffel bag, which he left in the truck as he rushed to the garage's side entrance. It took him no time to realize that the brick had been recently dusted off.

Motherfuck. He's here.

Ricky walked back into the garage and closed the side door behind him. He kept his golf clubs in the garage and pulled his nine iron out of the bag before continuing to the entrance to the house.

He tapped the button on the wall to close the garage door, its motor moaning as the door creaked shut.

No easy ways out. Ricky jiggled his key into the main door and pushed it open to a warm gust of air. He never left the heater running when he was away. Now he knew Jeremy was staying in his house.

Ricky kicked off his shoes as he entered the mud room, wanting to sneak through the house as quietly as possible. He tiptoed into the living room and saw the TV remote on the couch. He always left the remote on the TV stand.

Ricky crossed the living room into the kitchen, golf club firm in his two-fisted grip, ready to swing at any surprise. As if he needed further confirmation, Ricky opened the cabinets, praying to see his stock of food and snacks untouched.

He could've just stopped by, grabbed some things and left. If he stayed here, then all my food will be gone.

Ricky found what he feared: two depleted cabinets. There was nothing left but a box of trail mix and a bag of cashews, two things he knew Jeremy hated.

He opened the fridge behind him to find the milk was nearly empty; he knew for a fact there had been at least three quarters left when he had departed for the cabin.

"Fuck."

Every small creak in the house, every howl of the wind called his full attention as he stepped cautiously toward the living room.

"Jeremy?" he called, not expecting a response.

Ricky felt like he was starring in his own horror movie, moving stealthily through his house to avoid the killer. He'd never considered that he might be afraid of Jeremy, but that was how he had started to feel. The officer who had called him at the cabin had all but admitted that the press had made up the fact that Jeremy was armed and dangerous. It was highly unlikely he was armed, but dangerous? He did shoot dozen of his coworkers in cold blood. Who was to say he wouldn't turn on his own family?

My gun.

Ricky bolted up the stairs to his bedroom, running straight for the closet and tossing the golf club aside. He pulled open the closet door with trembling arms and fumbled through the mountain of dirty clothes, swimming through them until he located his M-16 case. He placed it on his bed, his shaky fingers having a hard time holding steady on the latches.

After fighting through the fidgeting, the case's lid popped open. Ricky could feel his heart pounding in his head.

"Jesus Christ," he whispered. His vision pulsed as he stared into the empty case.

Jeremy had stolen his military-issued assault rifle from his bedroom.

His mind flooded with possibilities. Was Jeremy planning another attack? Was he going to get revenge on someone? Did he want a gun for protection while he was on the run? Regardless, a fully automatic weapon in the hands of a mass murderer was bad news for everyone.

"What the fuck are you up to?" Ricky asked the empty case. The officer had mentioned he'd left a business card on his front door. Ricky ran back down the stairs and swung open the front door to find the card taped to the screen door. He snatched it and pulled out his cell phone to call Officer Ellis Reeves of the Denver Police Department.

The officer's cell phone number was circled, so Ricky called that.

"This is Reeves," the man answered after one ring.

"Hello, Officer, this is Ricky Heston."

"Mr. Heston, good afternoon. What can I do for you?" The officer's voice was distant and distracted.

"I'm afraid my nephew may have been at my house. My rifle is missing."

There was a moment of silence. "You're sure it couldn't have been anyone else? Or perhaps you misplaced it?"

"I'm positive. No one besides my immediate family even knows about the rifle—and none of them are around. It has to be Jeremy. He also knew where my spare key was hidden outside. Everyone else has moved away. It's him."

"I'll be there in five."

37

Chapter 37

Jeremy had already left Ricky's house the night before his uncle showed up in a panic. He had parked the car seven blocks away from the park, at a busy Burger King restaurant. It would likely take a day or two before anyone noticed it staying in the same spot and called for a tow truck. He left it unlocked, the keys on the passenger seat, should someone else want to come along and steal the vehicle; it was certainly the right neighborhood for such a possibility.

The stress he had felt from leaving Ricky's house and driving away had faded. Walking through the park with his backpack strapped on was his first real test in quite some time. He had debated fetching the car and bringing it back to his uncle's house, but decided it was too risky, even in the middle of the night. The car had been right where he left it in the park's parking lot, apparently drawing zero attention over the last few days. Apparently no one in Pueblo had made the connection between Jeremy and the stolen Chrysler, or else there would've been a statewide hunt for the vehicle.

Jeremy had tried to run across the park, but the backpack was too bulky and weighed heavily down on him, leaving him no choice but to walk at a regular pace. When he reached the car, he tossed the backpack into the passenger seat, knowing its size would give the appearance of a person riding shotgun. Constantly checking over his shoulder, Jeremy wasted no time in firing up the car and disappearing into the night.

His eyes were glued to the rearview mirror on the drive to downtown, but once he parked and stepped foot in downtown Denver, his soul felt rejuvenated. Even at midnight, a line formed around the Burger King drive-through, as he unloaded his bag from the stolen Chrysler.

Jeremy started walking, invisible in the night. The temperature had dropped into the upper thirties, but his layers of clothing kept him warm. Sleeping would be a different story, but he'd deal with that when the time came.

Walking down the nearly deserted streets of downtown Denver, Jeremy felt he could see his entire life when he looked behind him. The rows of streetlights glowed like orbs, stretching as far as he could see.

He thought of all the milestones and achievements he had reached in his life, and with each passing streetlight he remembered something else from his past.

He remembered being a child, growing up in his parents' now-abandoned house. All the times he had run around the backyard, pretending to be Batman and taking on the villains of the world. Going to his grandmother's house two blocks away, every day after school, for dinner, and her constant encouragement and support.

"You're gonna do big things in this world, peanut," she would tell him as a little boy, and he believed her still to this day.

Growing up with a loving family was something he never

took for granted, and he knew he could attribute much of his drive and success to that. His family now probably wondered where it all went wrong, but Jeremy didn't see it that way. Sure, he did a bad thing, but the reasons behind it were pure and intended to help way more people than it hurt.

He thought back to high school, those ever-important formative years when he was first exposed to psychology in an introductory class. He had signed up for it on a whim because his girlfriend at the time said he should. Had that never happened, would he be where he was today?

It was impossible to know, but he assumed likely not. Studying the human mind had sparked a passion unlike anything before. Learning about schizophrenia and many other mental disorders drove him to find out more and more. He'd always heard stories about his great-grandfather, but the family never went into detail. He was shunned, and they were ashamed. If they wouldn't give Jeremy the details, he'd have to learn about it on his own.

While he never had the chance to see his great-grandfather's medical file, he was able to piece together a picture of what he imagined the old man was going through: days spent in a padded room, deemed a danger to himself and the public.

He was exactly the kind of person Jeremy desperately wanted to help by carrying out his shooting. Great-Grandpa Heston never had a chance at a reformed life. In his day, mentally ill patients were treated like animals, locked up in rooms to be fed and bathed on a schedule. Doctors would try to understand the *why* behind the illness, but wouldn't bother curing the problems.

Treatment had evolved a lot since then, but a long road waited ahead. While hospitals now treated patients like human beings, Jeremy had witnessed firsthand that a proactive approach to healing the minds of patients was absent.

Dr. Carpenter had conducted extensive interviews with Jeremy, all targeted around learning *why* he had turned to violence. She prescribed pills to keep him lazy, but that only worked for so long once he caught on. Being in the mental hospital undercover gave Jeremy an edge in knowing what to look out for. He had learned in college that medication was always prescribed to patients. Keeping the patients unable to think for themselves kept the peace, and he couldn't blame them for that. If they let the patients run loose and act on their own accord, situations would escalate quickly and out of control.

At some point in college, Jeremy decided he was all-in for a future as a psychologist. Most people don't take the time to look back on their lives and connect the dots. Every decision made and every person met can lead to the next opportunity in life.

Jeremy appreciated this and traced his current situation back to that high school class. Everything from that point seemed to fall into place, to ensure he ended up here. Was it destiny or fate? Are we truly in control, or does one decision lead to the next, in a snowball effect, until we either look back at the damage or the good left behind?

He would never know for sure, but looking back at those streetlights kept his mind in awe of life. History would remember him as the man who killed thirteen of his coworkers only to be found not guilty by reason of insanity. His case would be studied in law schools all around the world as an example of how to achieve the unlikely verdict. Mental health professionals would point to his example, as to why mental health should be taken more seriously, and the opponents would forever scream for justice for the dead.

Despite his feeling just the day before that everything had turned out to be a lost cause thanks to the DA's blog, looking back at the last two years showed Jeremy the enormity of what he had accomplished. He likely wouldn't be alive to see the day where the mentally ill were regularly sentenced to hospitals instead of prisons, but he hoped to one day be looked back upon as the one who initiated the change.

A pioneer, he thought. It warmed him to know that he hadn't slain his friends for no reason. There was still progress that could be traced back to his case. Changing an entire society's outlook on such a sensitive matter was a near impossible task, but turning the figurative ship even one degree could put the future on an entirely different course. Hopefully history would look back at him as the one who moved things that one degree.

Jeremy approached the park that would serve as his home for the next two nights and thought how all of his choices had led to this moment. He didn't have much of a choice: he could either risk being caught and turned back over to the authorities, or hide out as long as possible, which meant sleeping in the park. There were at least fifteen others camped out for the night, some in sleeping bags, others on benches with layers of blankets stacked on them, and a couple of tents posted in the middle of the grass. How many of these people had no other choice? Surely their circumstances weren't as drastic as Jeremy's, but life had a funny way of leading you down its own path.

Keep your head down and talk to nobody. The last thing Jeremy wanted was to be shanked for his belongings and left to bleed out in the grass. Maybe that was a stereotype toward homeless people and unfair to judge, but he didn't want to find out. *Stereotypes exist because they're true.*

All the benches appeared occupied, so Jeremy tiptoed through the grass until he found a spot under a tree that had remained vacant after everyone else claimed their territory. He had no sleeping bag, and only a couple of blankets. The night would turn colder as he lay on the stiff ground, but he'd be warm enough to survive.

The grass crunched beneath the weight of his body as he lay on the ground. His backpack thumped as he dropped it; he lay it flat, to serve as his pillow. The heavy jacket provided warmth, but he pulled out the two blankets he had packed and pulled them over the length of his body.

The cloudless black sky above watched over him as Jeremy slept outdoors for the first time in his life.

38

Chapter 38

On Friday, Officer Reeves arrived to Ricky's house with a coffee cup in hand. He would've normally been on his way home for the evening, but the manhunt for Jeremy Heston called for all officers to put in overtime until he was captured. The police department didn't need another scene like the one they had to clean up two years ago.

Ricky opened the front door before the officer had walked up, and waited for him at the screen door.

"Good afternoon, Mr. Heston. How are you holding up?" Officer Reeves asked as he stepped inside the house.

Ricky stood tall at six feet, but he had to look up a few inches to meet Officer Reeves's fearless brown eyes. The officer was a bulky black man, muscles bulging from his dark blue uniform.

"I'm in shock, and freaking out." Ricky made no effort to hide the wavering in his voice.

"Understandable. I'm sure you have already, but may I take a look around the house?" Officer Reeves rubbed his bald, perfectly round head.

"Of course. My rifle was in my bedroom closet. Nothing else looks out of place from what I can tell."

"Thank you. Would you mind turning on your computer for me?"

"Sure thing."

Officer Reeves searched the bedroom first, looking for anything that might suggest where Jeremy had gone—but he'd covered his tracks pretty well. After a brief tour around the rest of the house, the officer met Ricky in his office.

"Can you please open your Internet browsing history? You said you were gone for a week, right? It's possible Jeremy left behind a trail on your computer."

"You got it." Ricky sat down in his chair, feeling his guts bubbling within. He hadn't considered checking the computer, and now he braced himself for what he might find. Ricky opened his Internet browser, Officer Reeves breathing steadily over his shoulder, and pulled up the history.

Dozens of websites had been visited over the last few days, and Ricky felt his palms turn clammy as he scrolled through the list.

"Looks like a lot of Google searches," Officer Reeves said, his voice sounding distant to Ricky.

"He searched himself," Ricky said. "It was one of the first things he looked up. If he didn't know he was famous, he sure does now." Ricky's voice spoke the words, but his mind could barely form a solid thought. "Holy shit."

Ricky pointed at the screen.

"The Taste of Denver," Officer Reeves said, unease now in his voice. "That starts tonight. Excuse me for a minute."

Ricky kept scrolling as Officer Reeves called his dispatcher, asking for reinforcements to be sent to the festival, which was starting in two hours.

"Not only was he looking at the event, he did a map search

of the surrounding blocks," Ricky said.

"He's planning another attack. That goddamn shrink was full of shit!"

"I'm sorry, who?"

"The doctor at Jeremy's hospital. Told us that Jeremy would no longer have violent urges, that the public would be in no danger. Psychologists just make shit up, I swear. Don't get me started." The officer started for the door, Ricky following behind.

"I need to get back to the station now, Mr. Heston. Leave your computer on and we'll remote in to see if our forensics can dig up anything more about Jeremy's plans. I'll be in touch."

Ricky nodded as the front door slammed shut, then went back to his office, sitting helpless at his computer. "God damn it, Jeremy. Where did we go so wrong with you?"

He left the computer on and grabbed his truck keys. *I'm gonna stop him before anyone else gets hurt.*

* * *

Hundreds, if not thousands, of people filled the streets of downtown Denver. Traffic sat at a standstill, road closures making it impossible to get across the city. Ricky sat in his truck and waited for the lines of vehicles to move forward.

The festival was at Civic Center Park, a few steps from the Colorado State Capitol, in the heart of the city. Ricky found a parking spot near the capitol, admiring its golden dome.

What am I even going to do? Find him and tackle him?

He didn't know, but Ricky felt he'd do anything to stop

another massacre. It was his responsibility. As a former Marine, stopping terrorists was what he was trained to do, and at the moment his own nephew posed a legitimate terror threat. With his own M-16.

Every time he thought about Jeremy taking the rifle from his closet, he shook his head in disgust. Jeremy really must have gone off the deep end to think any of this was alright. "Was killing thirteen people not good enough?" Ricky asked his empty truck.

He popped a few quarters into the meter, and worked his way toward the park.

Crowds lined the sidewalks around the capitol, many making their way to the festival, others stopping and taking pictures of the tri-level gray building and its golden dome.

Jeremy likely had no plans to actually enter the festival. The security team would have been informed to be on the lookout for Jeremy—but even without this new intel, Jeremy would know that the cops were out looking for him. He would be laying low, Ricky felt sure of it.

The festival wasn't even open yet, but herds of people were still lined up at its entrance, food trucks and tents visible to the hungry patrons on the other side of the chain-link fence.

Ricky's phone buzzed in his pocket, a call from an unknown number.

"Mr. Heston, we see you, and you need to leave the festival right now," Officer Reeves said before Ricky could greet him. "We're on it and don't need you in the line of danger."

The officer's tone insulted Ricky. "I fought in Desert Storm. I'm not worried about the line of danger, *Officer*. This is my nephew anyway. He won't hurt me."

"Mr. Heston. You're currently unarmed. Your nephew killed

some of his closest friends, just two years ago. It's wrong to think you're safe. You need to leave."

"No, thanks." Ricky ended the call and forced his way through the crowd.

39

Chapter 39

While his uncle and several undercover officers roamed the festival grounds, Jeremy lay on the grass at the park, hands crossed beneath his head while he gazed at the sky turning orange as the sun set. The day was warm, which would help with his final night of sleep in the outdoors. Jeremy knew that tomorrow night he would be sleeping in a jail, a hospital, or the morgue. The thought of death was growing like a fungus on his conscience.

He tried to focus on the task at hand. Doing something for a second time around felt easier and less nerve-wrecking. Two years ago, Jeremy remembered, he couldn't sleep, thousands of possibilities running through his mind as he considered his daunting task.

This time, the only real difficulty was coming to terms with the unknown. Jeremy had spent the entire day on the park bench, admiring the life that filled the park. Friends had picnics and played games, families went for an afternoon stroll, and the homeless wandered around in search of money for their next meal.

Everyone had a path in life that had led to this exact moment in the park. At the end of the day, life is nothing but a series of accidents that shape us as people.

Jeremy knew more people would lose their lives tomorrow, but would it be worth anything this time? He had learned that some things were simply out of his control. No matter how detailed a plan he laid out, the external factors were impossible to plan for. There would probably not be any drastic breakthrough or revelation—it would be just another mass shooting, with more dead bodies to add to the ever-growing tally.

But this time would be different—there had never been a repeat mass shooter. The stakes would be higher. A new trial would almost certainly end in an easy death penalty sentence; however, with an insanity verdict already delivered once, that could complicate the matter. Hospital security and protocol would be restructured to make sure something like this never happened again.

Jeremy could feel history in his grip, daring him to move forward, tempting him to leave a mark that would never be forgotten.

His actions would make the world a better place, and that was all he'd ever wanted. Nothing had really changed after the last time—this time it would be different. Perhaps that's what the other homeless people in the park were telling themselves as well.

Jeremy had considered walking around the festival to scope the area, but decided to spend his day at the park, knowing it was his last full day of breathing fresh city air, a free man's air.

* * *

Later Friday night, at 10:30, Officer Reeves sat at his desk, relieved. Jeremy had so far made no appearance at the Taste of Denver, and none of the officers patrolling the grounds had seen anything suspicious. "One night down, two to go," he told the deputy in charge of the case.

The forensics team had finished looking through Ricky Heston's computer and agreed there was a high probability that Jeremy was planning another shooting at the festival—though they'd gotten no insight into *when* Jeremy planned to open fire. The police chief had called for a higher presence both inside and outside the festival.

Officer Reeves had proposed that the chief release a state-ment to the public, informing them of Jeremy's possible plans for the weekend-long event.

The chief had responded, "The last thing we need, Reeves, is for citizens to be on edge at a fun event. If we released a statement, people might feel the need to be vigilant and bring guns with them downtown. We don't need that. We'll have enough officers at the event to stop any threat."

Officer Reeves hoped Jeremy wouldn't find a way to slip through the cracks and leave another grisly scene behind him. He was asked to lead the force patrolling Civic Center Park for the weekend, and spent the entire day reading through the massive file on Jeremy. He wanted to find anything that would provide insight into Jeremy's train of thought, but came up empty-handed. He had studied the route from Ricky's house to the festival, in search of possible locations Jeremy could hide. There were dozens, too many to check them all. Heston could have been halfway to Montana by now for all they knew—but

Reeves knew better.

Heston was a bipolar egomaniac and would want nothing more than to be in the limelight again.

Officer Reeves studied the areas surrounding Civic Center Park, circling every spot that would be prime for shooting into crowds. He assigned an officer to each circled area, for the rest of the festival.

"All hands on deck," he wrote in an email to the special team. "Some of us remember what this monster did two years ago, and we must use any means necessary to ensure it doesn't happen again. If you see him with a weapon, shoot him on sight."

The police chief had approved this decision as well, and was ready to back it up if needed—although he doubted the citizens of Denver would take any issue with Jeremy Heston catching a bullet to the head. Except for, perhaps, the twelve jurors who let him go.

Something in his gut told Officer Reeves that Jeremy would try to make his move on Saturday. It would be the highest-traffic day, and the only day of the festival that spanned from morning to night. It provided Jeremy the best opportunity to try something.

We'll be ready. Show your face. We'll be there.

Officer Reeves shut down his computer and left for the night, a few hours of uneasy sleep awaiting him.

40

Chapter 40

When the sun rose on Saturday morning, sparkling the dew on the park grass, Jeremy felt the same sense of destiny he'd had two years earlier. The air stood still, and the park remained silent, aside from the sporadic snores of the other homeless tenants. The nearby road was deserted, odd for a Saturday morning, especially with the festival opening less than a mile away at ten o'clock.

He dismissed the silence and prepared his mind for the task ahead. The M-16 rested stiffly in the backpack, which he squeezed to feel its calming presence. "Let's change the world some more," he whispered, rubbing his shoulder from the random throbs of pain still present.

Jeremy's stomach growled angrily. He hadn't eaten since yesterday afternoon when he finished the last of the snacks he'd brought from his uncle's house. A McDonald's was across the street, and he considered begging for a dollar to buy a burger, but decided against it. Too risky. Jeremy packed his blankets, stuffing them around the concealed rifle, and slung the backpack around his shoulders before crossing the street to the McDonald's.

When he entered, he saw a couple other homeless people sitting near the fireplace along the back wall, munching on their breakfast sandwiches as they stared out the window. The smell of sausage and pancakes filled the restaurant. He had frequented McDonald's two or three times a week as a broke college student, and the aroma caused an instant nostalgia for the days when life was simple.

He kept his head low and stared at the ground. It wasn't every day that someone who had murdered thirteen people in the community walked into a McDonald's for breakfast. Hopefully no one would notice and cause a scene.

Jeremy walked to the back of the restaurant, maintained a safe distance from his fellow homeless friends. He slid into a side booth that overlooked the park he had slept in. He couldn't believe the last week of his life. The odds of escaping a mental hospital were already slim to none, but making it from Pueblo to Denver with a police force and the public all on the lookout was flat-out amazing.

Maybe this is fate, Jeremy thought. Nothing else could explain him executing a once-in-a-lifetime mission. The verdict still felt like a dream he never woke up from. There were cases in the past where defendants had received the insanity verdict—but to receive it after the severity of the crime he'd committed made Jeremy feel like a supernatural force was guiding his life.

Maybe a book is still a good idea after all. After today, the story I have to tell will only be more bizarre.

The thought sparked in Jeremy a slight motivation boost. Crazier things had already occurred on this journey, so who knew what would happen?

Jeremy had gone to Taste of Denver as a teenager, and remembered that Saturday around noon was chaotic, lunchtime.

Noon would be the time for his attack. Four hours from now.

As he had hoped, a man in a jogging suit left a tray of half-eaten food on a table nearby. Once he confirmed the man was outside, Jeremy shuffled over to the tray and picked up the remaining hash browns, coffee, and one pancake. People could always be counted on to leave food behind, no matter the restaurant.

A whole park full of food trucks and I'm scraping for people's leftovers.

He scarfed the remains and felt the food settle into his starving gut, which groaned in delight. By the time he sucked the hash brown's salt off his fingers, a new wave of energy had entered Jeremy.

Today is a beautiful day for making history.

When he stepped outside the restaurant, the sun had completely risen and shone warmly over the city. It was one of those spring mornings in Denver that felt more like a summer morning. The day would be hot, probably in the seventies, while the night would bring a chill. Fortunately, he'd be back in a jail cell and wouldn't have to worry about staying warm.

Bicyclists sped by on the street, and cars made their way toward Civic Center Park. People strolled down the sidewalk, one with a family pushing two infants in a double stroller.

Don't shoot any kids today. Jeremy made this mental note. It hadn't been an issue the last time, since the shooting occurred in his workplace. He took a deep breath and let the fresh air fill his lungs—a burst of life he hadn't felt in years.

He crossed the street back to the park, planning to wait out the next couple of hours there before heading to Civic Center Park. Once the crowds started to form, he would find a spot on the capitol's lawn to post up until it was time for action.

There would be thousands of people and no one would pay any attention to a bum enjoying the sunny day.

His bench from earlier remained vacant, so Jeremy lay his backpack next to it and sat. A black and yellow butterfly landed on his backpack and past memories flooded his mind—one in particular that had been pushed back into the furthest depths of his memories.

It was the first time in 20 years that he'd thought about his little sister's gruesome death, and he wasn't sure why it had been so long. Thinking back, he couldn't clearly remember the event, but ony that it had happened. He had watched as she chased a butterfly into the street and was hit by a car in front of their house.

In the months following her death, Jeremy had spent every night vomiting into the toilet, the images and sounds of her crushed body never leaving his mind. His parents had scheduled a series of meetings with Dr. Morgan—Jeremy's first encounter with a shrink, which likely contributed to his interest in psychology.

Dr. Morgan had taken Jeremy through a rigorous program where they focused on erasing the memory of the accident. Jeremy's parents had been concerned that this system would completely erase his sister's existence from his memory—which it did—but it was better than watching him go through a physical pain that refused to fade away in the initial months after the accident.

Jeremy couldn't deny that it worked; he never thought about his sister or her accident. Even during his interviews for the trial, the memory had been so far gone that he never thought of mentioning it. It was like that painful day had been erased and recorded over like an old VHS tape.

"Why are you coming to me today of all days?" he asked the butterfly. "Leave me alone to do what I need to do."

The butterfly ignored him and remained still on the backpack.

In an attempt to keep his mind distracted from history, pounding at the door of his mind, he watched the groups of people walking along the park, all of them headed in the direction of the festival.

41

Chapter 41

At 11:30, Jeremy broke out of his daydreams. His attempt to avoid thinking of the past had been a failure. Instead, he had mentally traced his current predicament back as far as possible. While there were some scenarios that stretched back to childhood events, most pointed to his monthly meetings with Dr. Siva at the university.

Having fun in jail, old friend? Jeremy wondered. He had gone through too much with Dr. Siva, who now haunted his mind whenever he closed his eyes. He had played Jeremy like an instrument, manipulating his mind into believing all of this was okay. The thing that pissed Jeremy off the most was that he *still* believed it, unable to shake the thought, as if his brain had been rewired to ignore his conscience.

He also wondered what Dr. Carpenter was doing these days. What did she think of his escape, so shortly after her dismissal? Was this all some sort of conspiracy to help Jeremy escape?

He knew he shouldn't be worrying about these things, which were out of his control, but Jeremy's mind couldn't resist. It was trying to slow him down, prevent him from carrying out the task ahead.

His thoughts kept him company on his long walk down the sidewalk. His back became sticky with sweat, the temperature increasing by the minute. The blankets in the backpack added more weight and slowed him down. Being homeless required being in shape, apparently. The exercises he had done in jail and the hospital had not been enough to prepare him for this, especially with his shoulder still on the mend.

Jeremy felt nerves, but not the adrenaline he had hoped for. Adrenaline would have given him a boost he could've really used on this hot day. The day of the office shooting, he had felt like he was running on clouds when he sprinted around the office building to barricade the doors. His hands didn't even have their usual tremble when he thought about shooting his gun, and he wondered if he had grown numb to the sensation of it all.

Focus. Focus. Focus. Jeremy didn't like the direction his mind was trying to go. *You may not be as prepared as last time, but you're still a good shot. Nothing to worry about, it's like riding a bike.* It was Doomsday part two, and the time had finally come to pull his head out his ass and get the job done.

He paid no attention to the other people lining the sidewalk, and as he approached the Burger King from two nights ago, his heart sunk when he saw the car he had stolen was gone.

If the police found it, they could be on to me. I shouldn't have parked it anywhere near the festival. I should've parked two miles away and walked. Stupid.

"Just keep going," he told himself and put his head down.

Five minutes later, he stood at Lincoln Street, in front of the capitol building. Red brick stairs led up to a platform lined with brick and stone pavers that formed a circle around a statue of a Civil War Union soldier. Behind the statue stood the capitol, with towering dark stone columns that all led up to a shining, golden dome, reflecting the sun in every direction.

Jeremy stared at the building in awe. Colorado had been his only home in his 26 years of life. It was fitting that the capitol would be one of the last things he'd see before being shut in the dark for the rest of his life. His name would forever be etched into the state's history, if it wasn't already, and the sentiment made him grin.

Behind him, the park swarmed with people, food trucks, and large white tents. The murmur of chatter filled the air as a quick glance suggested at least 200 people in the immediate vicinity of the capitol steps, not counting the other bystanders spread across sidewalks and grassy areas, and the stopped cars on Lincoln Street, sitting like ducks.

"See, everything is going to be fine. There are plenty of lives to change." A woman who had been snapping pictures of the capitol with her phone gave Jeremy a curious look when he spoke to himself. Homeless people liked to talk to themselves, in Jeremy's experience, so hopefully that only added to his disguise. The woman scurried away to her group of friends.

Jeremy sat down on a bench that faced the Civil War statue and watched the hundreds of people across the street, waiting in line to enter the festival.

42

Chapter 42

Officer Reeves patrolled the blocks surrounding the festival. Laughter and the hum of hundreds of conversations filled the air as he kept close to the chain-link fence surrounding Civic Center Park—and he intended to keep it that way. Screams would be bad, gunshots would be a nightmare come true.

Personally, he felt overwhelmed, having to examine every person who passed by. His senses throbbed on high alert and adrenaline dripped constantly into his bloodstream. He had to remind himself that he wasn't on this mission alone; there were fifteen other officers, both inside and outside the festival, looking up, down, and for anything out of the ordinary.

The unknowing kept him on edge. He had deployed his team of officers based on a hunch that Jeremy would try to strike today. No evidence backed up his claim, yet no one questioned it. Everyone, including the chief of police, wanted to take no risks and understood the gravity of what could happen.

Even if they went the whole weekend without a disturbance, Officer Reeves would consider it a success. Their presence alone could factor into Jeremy's hesitation to pull the trigger again.

The other officers kept an open flow of communication on the radio. Jeremy's code name was Hitchcock, a reference to the director's horror film *Psycho*. So far there had been no sighting of "Hitchcock," and each passing minute made Officer Reeves both more uneasy and more relieved.

He had emphasized that the team not overreact. "Be 100 percent confident in your decisions today. One misstep can cause chaos. People are here for a good time. We're not here to spread fear, we're here to make sure they have that good time."

Everyone understood and no questions were asked. With the team all on the same page, they spread across the festival grounds, some undercover, some in uniform.

Officer Reeves could see his team as he paced along the fence. Everyone was assigned a specific zone, while he roamed throughout them all.

If Heston were to show up with an M-16, how could he not be noticed? That's a big rifle.

The question had been posed the day before, in a brainstorming session with the rest of the special force. It would be impossible for him to enter the festival with it, as there were metal detectors at the entrance. It being a chain-link fence, though, meant it wouldn't be impossible for someone to climb over it. Insanity could make a man do anything, though, and jumping a fence seemed elementary compared to what Heston had already done. Every officer on the outside of the festival had eyes on the fence, looking for anyone who might try to make the jump.

Everyone remained on the lookout for someone with extralarge bags, one too many layers, or someone watching the park from afar. With thousands of people flooding the now-closed streets surrounding the park, there were hundreds of people who met this criteria.

"Remember to keep an eye for people by themselves, keeping a short distance from the park. Anyone at all looking in the direction of the festival," Officer Reeves said into his radio on his shoulder. He remembered another key note from his research the night before. "Hitchcock is known to have a distant look on his face. Watch for someone staring, but not really seeing."

The afternoon heat increased, and combined with the grills and ovens running all day, the park felt like a heat wave had been released into it. Officer Reeves wiped the sweat off his temple and kept walking toward the entrance. The buildings surrounding the park would require access that Jeremy simply couldn't have obtained in such a short time span. Sure, he was smart, but there was no way he'd have been able to pull that off, especially with the whole city knowing he was on the run.

As he approached the entrance, a lady screamed in the distance, likely from inside the festival. His first instinct sent his hand to the pistol on his utility belt, but he left it there when laughter broke out immediately following the shriek.

The day had him on tilt, and all he could do was take it one minute at a time.

His cell phone buzzed in his pocket and he snapped it out in a quick motion.

"This is Reeves," the officer answered after one ring.

"Officer, this is Ricky Heston. I have an update for you." Ricky spoke with a slight tremble.

"This better help us find your nephew."

"I think it might. I've spent all morning going through my things and it appears my hunting backpack is missing. I'm positive Jeremy took it to carry my M-16."

"Describe it, please. Color, size, anything unique," Officer Reeves said quickly.

"It's about three feet tall, one of those oversize backpacks. It's camouflage, for hunting. It might look extra big on him, since he's much smaller than me."

"Perfect, thank you for the information. Call me with anything else." Officer Reeves hung up and immediately radioed the update to the rest of the team.

The voice of Officer Santiago crackled across the airwaves. "I see someone with that backpack. On the capitol steps, by the statue."

Officer Reeves's heart pounded harder. "What's he wearing?" Reeves demanded.

"He looks homeless. Some sweatpants, baggy coat, a beanie, and the backpack at his side."

Shit, Reeves thought. *That could be any bum off the streets.* The last thing he needed was a dead, innocent homeless man. He had to be sure.

"What's he doing?" Reeves asked.

"Nothing," Santiago responded, sounding unsure of himself. "I mean, he's just sitting on the bench, looking around."

"Is he looking in the direction of the park?"

"Kind of. He's looking all around. I'm not sure at what."

"Keep an eye on him. Get as close as you can without revealing yourself. Everyone else stay ready for my word, I'm heading over there."

43

Chapter 43

Jeremy sat on the bench, his stomach doing cartwheels as he anticipated the next few minutes.

It's time.

Not having a set plan sparked his anxiety, and his neck had tensed up as a result. He rolled his head in every direction to try and relieve the tension.

Last time, he'd planned on being caught and taken to jail. This time, however, he could make a run for it, should he choose to. The crowd would erupt into chaos, making it easy for him to blend in and run away with everyone else. How would the police know who to look for in a panicked stampede?

Jeremy looked up at the perfect blue sky and took a deep inhale, getting a whiff of all kinds of food he couldn't decipher. *Enjoy it, because if they catch you they'll never let you out of your room again.*

His mental memory reel had finally run out. There were no more memories to reflect on. The last two years had been filled with hours upon hours to reminisce on the past—which he did, but nothing compared to how much he had the last two days. He had come to peace with the fact that his old life would officially be left in the rearview, his family would no longer speak of him, and he would be erased from their memories, like his great-grandfather had been.

Jeremy also knew that his book idea would probably never come to fruition—barring another act of God. The book was supposed to be the end result of this whole experiment. Instead, the experiment led him to a dead end.

"How do you get out of a dead end?" he asked himself in a low whisper. "You either turn around, or die. That's why it's called a *dead* end."

How sentimental, his inner voice chimed in. *Never knew you could be such a romantic after Jamie left you out to dry.*

Jeremy no longer gave a shit what his inner voice had to say, and he smirked at the thought of Jamie. If only someone would tell you how life would end up, then maybe you really would enjoy living in the moment. His relationship with Jamie, during the good times, was the happiest he had ever felt. Smelling her scent, feeling her warmth on a cold night, hearing her laughter late into the night as they stayed up watching TV.

If you had put as much effort into that relationship as you did into pretending to be crazy, you might have a totally different life today. Your best friend could be your wife that you come home to every day and talk about how much you hate your job, and she would still love you. Hell, you might even have had kids by this point. A family with Jamie, all down the drain.

"Fuck you," he said through a swollen throat, holding back tears.

Fuck me? This was all your decision. I've only been along for the ride, to say what your heart truly desires.

"She'll remember me. Both as I was, and for what I did to change the world."

Ha! She thinks you're a nutcase, which you are, but whatever you need to tell yourself to sleep at night.

"Enough!" Jeremy yelled, causing a group of people nearby to stop mid-conversation and turn to him, gawking in disgust at the homeless man.

Jeremy stood from the bench and hunched over the backpack to unzip it. The barrel of the M-16 poked out like an erection from the darkness inside the bag, and he grabbed it to pull out the rifle.

A woman in the group nearby gasped and started to run. "He's got a gun!" The others with her shrieked and joined her in running the opposite direction, but no one else nearby paid any attention. Everyone was too busy carrying on in their own worlds to care what was happening on the capitol steps.

Jeremy reached a hand into the backpack and grabbed a couple of the extra magazines, dropping them on the ground beside him as he rotated to face Civic Center Park.

The sidewalk below swarmed with people, still unaware of what was going on above them. Across Lincoln Street was the festival, and at least a couple thousand people were packed into the space that stretched a quarter-mile into the distance.

The world came to a standstill as he pulled the rifle over his shoulder and let it fall into his grip, the barrel in his left hand and his right index finger sliding naturally over the trigger.

Jeremy peered into the scope, to ensure his aim was focused on a heavily populated area of the park. The nerves left his body, leaving him with a clear mind as he focused in on his target.

Two shots rang out before he could pull the trigger, and he was sent flying backward from what felt like a hard shove to the chest. His arms flailed as he tried to catch himself, sending the

233

M-16 into orbit. The rifle clattered to the ground at the same time his body hit the bricks behind him with a heavy thud.

He felt as if he were breathing fire with each inhale. A burning sensation filled his lungs. Jeremy lay on his back, his limbs splayed out in every direction. He heard footsteps clapping on the ground around him, moving away from him. Voices faded in and out, phrases he couldn't quite make out. He stared at that same blue sky above and saw a plane flying, leaving a white trail behind it. Footsteps approached, and a familiar face popped into his line of vision.

"You don't think it ends this way, do you?" the man in the black suit asked with a wide grin. His skin looked pale, almost matching his teeth. The sun reflected off his polished black shoes, blinding Jeremy for a moment while his eyes adjusted. The man giggled and knelt beside Jeremy's head.

Jeremy tried to speak, but his throat locked. His jaw clenched like a bear trap as his body started to tremble.

"Jeremy, Jeremy," the man said in an amused voice, patting Jeremy's chest. "Your body is entering a state of shock. You've been shot in the chest and arm, but you're going to be just fine. I know you wanted to come with me today, but I'm not quite ready for you."

Despite his numb body, Jeremy could now feel the warmth of blood spreading under his back, and he could *smell* the blood too.

"You won't see me again for a very long time," the man said. "Your road ahead is long, my friend, but you'll be back one day. Stronger than ever."

He reached down and touched Jeremy's shoulder with care. Flashbacks burst into his mind, each of the prior three times he had encountered the black-suited man: the Open Hands office, the jail cell, and the mental institution.

"You've done so much for me, Jeremy. Thank you. Until next time." The man removed his hand and Jeremy felt his breathing return to a less painful level; the burning sensation had fallen numb.

A young policeman appeared in his line of vision, blocking out the sun. Jeremy could see his lips moving, as if he was shouting, but there was no sound as his mind fell silent. He kept his eyes fixated on the sky and watched the bright blue fade as he fell into darkness.

44

Chapter 44

The days following Jeremy's shooting on the capitol steps were focused mainly on the hero: Officer Reeves. The man who stopped the country's next mass shooting was honored at events around the state, and even received a standing invitation for dinner at the White House.

Always a humble man, Officer Reeves continually gave credit to both Ricky Heston for the "phone call that saved the world" and to Officer Santiago, for spotting Jeremy across the street from the festival.

As the news made its way around the country, people continued their debates, going in circles around gun control and mental health. Jeremy had taken drastic actions to spark a conversation around mental health, which had slowly happened. Nothing had changed, but the motion was in place, and change was imminent.

Mental health advocates called for stronger security at hospitals and revised protocol for emergencies. As more details about Jeremy's escape came to light with each passing day, hospitals around the country vowed to review their policies and retrain staff on proper procedure. They added their voice, uniting to make sure that positive change would be implemented. The Rocky Mountain Health Institute, the center of the drama and one of the more renowned facilities in the world, committed to going back to the drawing board, to ensure this kind of thing never happened again.

Jeremy spent the following two weeks in the hospital, recovering from the gunshot wounds that refused to take his life. Media outlets from around the world swarmed the outside of the hospital for the first week, waiting with heavy anticipation for something to happen.

But nothing did. His parents had disappeared from the face of the planet. Jeremy had no statement to release, as he remained heavily guarded, with a police presence outside his hospital room door around the clock.

Word broke that Jeremy would have another trial, to begin in April. While there was immediate speculation that he could win another insanity verdict—he was already sentenced and diagnosed as insane, after all—the hype died down after Linda Kennedy announced she would not be defending Jeremy at his second trial.

News of the scam that Dr. Siva had managed to pull off never drew national attention, with Jeremy being shot and escaping during the same time frame. This time around, Jeremy would have no one in his corner. He'd have a public defender with no clue how to win such a high-profile insanity case. There'd be no money funneled to pay for top-ranking psychologists.

The district attorney's office announced that they would charge Jeremy with 200 counts of attempted murder—one for each round of ammunition in his possession—on top of violation of his court order, disturbing the peace, and grand theft auto.

Jeremy had plenty of time to reflect from his hospital bed, and knew he had no chance of escaping a prison sentence this time around. The death penalty was off the table, as he hadn't actually murdered anyone, but he knew the courts wouldn't allow him to be sent to the loony bin again. Not after what had nearly happened this last time.

He may have been diagnosed as bipolar, but Jeremy wasn't sure what to believe. He could acknowledge that he had moments where he felt like himself, and other times when he felt someone else might have taken over the wheel for a few moments. Regardless of what was happening within his mind, though, he smiled every night before falling asleep, knowing he had paved the way for future mentally ill patients to have a fighting chance in the court system.

Should he spend the rest of his life in a maximum-security prison, he would rest easy knowing he had done everything within his power.

Looking back, Jeremy realized just how far he had come. There were moments where it had felt like his entire plan would come crumbling down on him. Everything had to fall just the way it had, for him to end up in his current situation, and he wouldn't have changed a thing. Dr. Siva might have believed that he was the one pulling the strings, but Jeremy had done the dirty work, and put himself in the position to succeed. Maybe things would've ended up differently without his old professor's influence, but he'd never know. All he knew was that he had done what he could, until he reached the end result.

The world would continue to buzz about him outside of the hospital, outside of his prison. But Jeremy was a man at peace with all he had done. He carried his victims in his heart every day and thanked them for their sacrifice during his prayers every night. With the burden of his experiment finally lifted, Jeremy felt free for the first time in years.

Prison would do nothing to stop his freedom, either, because to him, freedom was more mental and emotional than physical. He no longer had to hide who he was or what he was up to. He could go back to being himself, and focus on his own inner peace. The light of day might never find him again, but he had brought light to those in need.

I did it. I changed the world.

Only time would tell if it was for better or worse.

Acknowledgements

Now that this series is done, it's time to reflect. I'd like to first thank my editor, Teja Watson, who helped keep this series on the right course and ensured everything flowed together from book to book. Your attention to detail will always be appreciated. Dane Low, my cover artist, for creating a consistent design that worked throughout the entire trilogy. My advanced readers team for helping along the way. The feedback you provide is always invaluable and the most meaningful. You are the first test run for any book, and you help shape it in more ways than you know. Maria Yates for giving additional insight, especially on the psychological matters. Arielle and Felix, somehow, whenever the writing gets slow or hard to push through, I just need to look at a picture of you two and know I need to keep moving forward. And lastly, my wife, Natasha, for helping shape the vision and being that first, brutally honest reader.

Enjoy this book?

You can make a difference!

Reviews are the most helpful tools in getting new readers for any books. I don't have the financial backing of a New York publishing house and can't afford to blast my book on billboards or bus stops.

(Not yet!)

That said, your honest review can go a long way in helping me reach new readers. If you've enjoyed this book, I'd be forever grateful if you could spend a couple minutes leaving it a review (it can be as short as you like) on the Amazon page. You can jump right to the page by clicking below.

US

UK

Thank you so much!

About the Author

Born in Denver, CO, Andre Gonzalez has always had a fascination with horror and the supernatural starting at a young age. He spent many nights wide-eyed and awake, his mind racing with the many images of terror he witnessed in books and movies. Ideas of his own morphed out of movies like *Halloween* and books such as *Pet Sematary* by Stephen King. These thoughts eventually made their way to paper, as he always wrote dark stories for school assignments or just for fun. *Followed Home* is his debut novel based off of a terrifying dream he had many years ago at the age of 12. His reading and writing of horror stories evolved into a pursuit of a career as an author, where Andre hopes to keep others awake at night with his frightening tales. The world we live in today is filled with horror stories, and he looks forward to capturing the raw emotion of these events, twisting them into new tales, and preserving a legacy in between the crisp bindings of novels.

Andre graduated from Metropolitan State University of Denver with a degree in business in 2011. During his free time, he enjoys baseball, poker, golf, and traveling the world with his family. He believes that seeing the world is the only true way to stretch the imagination by experiencing new cultures and meeting new people.

Andre still lives in Denver with his wife, Natasha, and tl two kids.

Made in the USA
Columbia, SC
06 September 2018